Mia
fashion
plates
and
cupcakes

SIMON SPOTLIGHT

An imprint of Simon & Schuster Children's Publishing Division
1230 Avenue of the Americas, New York, New York 10020
Copyright © 2014 by Simon & Schuster, Inc.
All rights reserved, including the right of reproduction
in whole or in part in any form.
SIMON SPOTLIGHT and colophon are registered
trademarks of Simon & Schuster, Inc.
Text by Tracey West
Chapter header illustrations by Maryam Choudhury
Designed by Laura Roode
For information about special discounts for bulk purchases, please contact
Simon & Schuster Special Sales
at 1-866-506-1949 or business@simonandschuster.com.
Manufactured in the United States of America 0114 OFF
First Edition 2 4 6 8 10 9 7 5 3 1
ISBN 978-1-4424-9790-0 (pbk)
ISBN 978-1-4424-9791-7 (hc)
ISBN 978-1-4424-9792-4 (eBook)
Library of Congress Catalog Card Number 2013954898

CUPCAKE DIARIES

Mia
fashion
plates
and
cupcakes

by coco simon

Simon Spotlight

New York   London   Toronto   Sydney   New Delhi

CHAPTER 1

We Are Such Pros!

"Do you need help with those, Katie?" I asked.

My friend Katie was carrying two cupcake carriers stacked on top of each other, and a bag of supplies dangled from her wrist. It made me a little nervous watching her. Katie is my BFF here in Maple Grove and I love her, but she's had some serious cupcake disasters before.

"No, I got it," Katie assured me. She carefully placed the carriers on our cupcake sales table and then looked around. "Wow, there's some cool stuff here."

We were inside the Maple Grove Women's Club, which may not sound superexciting, except that it was the day of their craft fair. Local artists and craftspeople were setting up tables with the stuff they'd made, like knitted scarves and hand-made beaded jewelry.

"Yeah, I hope we can look around a little," I said. "Alexis was really smart to suggest we set up here."

At that moment our friend Alexis walked up to us, carrying a notebook and a cash box.

"Did I just hear you say I was really smart?" she asked with a grin.

I nodded. "I never would have thought to sell cupcakes at a craft fair, but it's kind of a genius idea."

"Not genius, just obvious," Alexis said. "People who go to craft fairs get hungry. Besides, our cupcakes are handmade too, and they're like little works of art. I think the decorations and flavors you guys came up with are genius."

"Thanks," I said. I was pretty proud of what we had done. "We should get things set up before it starts."

My mom is a member of the Women's Club, so I had arrived early with her and started to set up the table. Once Alexis had suggested we sell at the craft fair, we came up with a theme: "Crafty Cupcakes."

Whenever we do an event, we have to plan out a bunch of things: what flavor to make the cupcakes; how to decorate the cupcakes; how to display the cupcakes; and how to decorate the table. For the craft fair, I thought we should stick with what people think of as traditional "cupcakey" colors— pink, mint green, light blue, and yellow. So the first thing I did was put down a pink tablecloth. We had used it for a baby shower once, and we like to reuse things to help with the costs.

Then I set up a backdrop, which I made from one of those big trifold cardboard displays that you can get for school projects. For the middle panel, I cut out letters from scrapbook paper to spell out "Crafty Cupcakes." The papers had little white flowers and dots on them, so it looked really cute. Then I had drawn some pictures of cupcakes along with pictures of crafty things, like paintbrushes and yarn and knitting needles.

On each side panel, I had printed out our Cupcake Club logo: a cupcake in a light blue wrapper with pink icing and a red cherry on top, and the words "cupcake" above it and "club" below. I had designed the logo myself at summer camp. We made T-shirts with the logo too, which we wore whenever we had a Cupcake event. Anyway, I stood up the backdrop at the back of the table, and then I was ready for the cupcake displays.

It's tempting to buy cool new stuff for our

displays each time, but then we wouldn't make as much profit. And Alexis is always talking about profit, since that's the money we get to keep. So we usually reuse what we can or make what we need. For this display, however, I bought some wooden cake stands from the craft store and painted them in our cupcakey colors. Then I added a clear, shiny coat so that it would be safe to put food on the stands. They looked really pretty on the table. They were on sale, and they were something we could use over and over again, so they were worth buying.

"I'll get the rest of the cupcakes from the car," Katie said, hurrying off.

"Mind if I set up the cash box?" Alexis asked.

"That's fine. I've got this," I said.

I slipped on some thin plastic gloves and opened up the first carrier. It contained our first batch of cupcakes: vanilla cake with vanilla icing, decorated with flowers made of fondant. Fondant is this paste made of sugar that you can roll out like dough and cut into shapes. We'd used pink and yellow for the flowers, so I put them on the green cake stand for a nice contrast.

The second carrier held our "yarn" cupcakes. We'd made red velvet cupcakes with cream cheese frosting. Then we'd used marzipan, which is a sugary almond paste that you can shape into stuff—kind of like edible modeling clay. We'd dyed it blue and then rolled it into little balls of "yarn," to go with the crafts theme. The yarn looked really cute sitting on top of the icing. I put those on the pink cake stand.

Katie came in carrying more cupcake carriers. The third held chocolate cupcakes with chocolate frosting. We'd decorated them with little jelly candies that we thought looked like jewels. For our fourth kind of cupcake, we had gone with one of our more adventurous flavors—lemon ginger— because a lot of people will buy a cupcake if it's a flavor they've never tried before. We'd topped them with pale-yellow lemon frosting and decorated them with birds.

I think I was most proud of the bird cupcakes, because I had experimented a lot to find the best way to do them. You know those old-fashioned candies that are shaped like leaves? I thought they kind of looked like birds' bodies. So I'd sliced them through the middle to make them thinner. Then I'd used little tubes of icing to draw on an eye, a beak, and wings, and I'd made swirly designs all around them. They looked really amazing.

Katie helped me put the rest of the cupcakes on

the stands, and then we stashed the carriers under the table. Alexis, Katie, and I stood in front of the table to see how everything looked.

"This might be our nicest display yet," Alexis remarked. "It's too bad Emma is not here."

Emma, the fourth member of the Cupcake Club, was off on a modeling job in the city.

"I'll send her a picture," Katie said, taking out her phone.

Alexis scrolled through the screen on her own smartphone. "So, display, check. Cupcakes, check. Business cards, check. Cash box, check. Flyers, check." She looked up at us. "Wow, I can't believe it. I think we're all set. We didn't forget anything."

I checked the time. "There's a few minutes before the doors open. I want to look around before it gets busy."

"I'll watch the table," Alexis offered.

"Thanks," Katie said. "I want to look around too."

So Katie and I walked around the room, checking out the crafts. Some of the stuff was kind of old-fashioned and looked like my grandma would like it, but some of it was really cool. We went to a table with beaded jewelry first, and Katie picked up a bracelet made out of chunky glass beads.

"This is so cool! The beads look like candy, almost," she said.

The woman setting up the booth smiled. "I call that my 'candy shop' style," she said, and then nodded to our shirts. "So, you're the girls from the cupcake stand?"

We nodded. "Yes," I said. "We started a cupcake club at school and turned it into a business."

"That's really ambitious," she said. "Good luck today!"

We thanked her and moved on to a table full of knitted scarves and then to another cool table with all these awesome animals and creatures sewn from felt. The girl behind it looked like she was in high school, and her blond hair was streaked with red and purple.

"These are sooo cute!" Katie squealed, picking up a little green squirrel with a goofy face.

"That's my favorite one," the girl said.

Katie dug into her jeans pocket and pulled out some bills. "I have to get this. You're coming home with me, Nutsy."

I laughed. "Nutsy?"

"Well, she's a squirrel, isn't she? And squirrels like nuts," Katie said.

"I think it's a good name for a squirrel," said the

girl, giving Katie her change. She also handed over a business card with the name Super Stuffies on it.

Then I noticed people were starting to come through the doors, so I tapped Katie on the arm.

"We'd better go help Alexis," I said.

When we got back to the table I saw a glamorous-looking woman with long black hair standing there. She wore black skinny jeans, black boots, and a black short-sleeved turtleneck. For a second I didn't recognize her.

"Hi, Mom," I said, running up to her. My mom always looks stunning, whether she's at the super-market or going out to eat at a hot restaurant in the city. You've always got to look good when you're a fashion stylist.

"Mia, the table looks lovely," Mom said. "You girls did a wonderful job."

"They certainly did."

A gray-haired woman walked up to us. She wore a long, flowy purple tunic over black leggings, which made her look very artistic.

"Mia, this is Mrs. Barrows, the president of the Women's Club," my mom said. "This my daughter and her friends Katie and Alexis."

Mrs. Barrows looked over the cupcake booth. "This is a lovely addition to our craft fair. I can't believe you girls made these cupcakes yourselves. They're beautiful!"

Alexis took a vanilla flower cupcake from the stand. "They taste as good as they look," she said, handing her one.

"Why, thank you!" Mrs. Barrows said. She unwrapped it and took a bite. "You're certainly right. This is delicious! You girls are quite professional."

Then two women walked up to our table, and we had to go into "sales mode," as Alexis would say. Katie and I answered questions about what was in each cupcake, and Alexis took the money, made change, and made sure everyone left with a business card and a flyer.

It was kind of a long day. We were pretty much busy the whole time, and we took turns leaving the table to eat the bagged lunches we had brought. Things finally slowed down in the afternoon.

Alexis put her hands on her hips, surveying the table. We had about two dozen cupcakes left. She looked around the room, counting.

"We should give one to each of the vendors," she said finally. "I don't think we'll sell out, and these are the kind of people who appreciate home-made things."

9

I'm always amazed by Alexis. It's like her mind is constantly churning out great business ideas.

"Let's do it," I agreed, and we took turns going to the tables and giving a cupcake to each vendor—along with a business card, of course. Everyone was really happy to get a cupcake.

We even had time to do a little shopping by the end of the day. I bought a really cool crocheted infinity scarf with black fringe along the edges, and when Katie wasn't looking, I went back to the jewelry table and got her the bracelet that looked like candy. I figured I'd save it for her birthday.

I also went back to the girl with the stuffies. One of her creatures was a little purple monster, and I thought Ethan might like it. He's the mostly-annoying-but-sometimes-cute son of Lynne, my dad's girlfriend.

"No charge," the girl said when I tried to pay. "That was an awesome cupcake."

"Wow, thank you," I said. "That's really nice of you."

When I got back to the table, Alexis was counting out the cash box.

"Except for the cupcakes we gave away, we sold them all," she said, looking at the clock, "with only five minutes to go. That's pretty perfect."

"Definitely," Katie agreed.

"Mrs. Barrows said we were professional," I reminded them. "Maybe she's right. I mean, it's like we've figured out how to smooth away all the problems we usually have."

"This *was* a pretty smooth event," Alexis agreed, "but there are always going to be problems That's just the way it is in a business."

"Maybe," I said. "But I'll keep my fingers crossed that things stay smooth."

Little did I know that things were about to get bumpier than lumpy cupcake frosting—but it wasn't the Cupcake Club's fault at all.

CRAFTY CUPCAKES

CHAPTER 2

Torn Between Two Clubs

The bumpiness started just two days later. After school, I went to Mrs. Kratzer's room for a staff meeting of the school newspaper, the *Park Street Times* (named after the school I go to, Park Street Middle School). I joined the staff a few months ago as a fashion reporter. The Cupcake Club keeps me busy, but it doesn't take me that long to write an article every week, and it's a subject I love.

I should also probably mention Chris Howard asked me to join. Emma loves to tease me that he's the reason I joined. There's this whole thing where we once went to a dance together, and we hang out sometimes, but I'm not officially allowed to date anyone so . . . whatever. He's really cute and nice. But he's not the *only* reason I joined, although

Emma will never believe that. She's so romantic.

When I got to the room, a bunch of kids were sitting at the long table in the back. Mrs. Kratzer, the paper's adviser, sat at her desk, grading papers. She doesn't like to run the meetings because she says we need to learn how to figure things out on our own, but she's there to answer questions if we need her.

It works out okay because the editor of the paper, Donovan Shin, is really organized. He reminds me a little of Alexis. When I sat down, he handed me a chart with a list of articles for the next issue of the paper. It showed what each article was about, who was writing it, and what date it was due.

Chris sat across the table from me, and he looked over and smiled. I smiled back. Chris has braces—the metal kind, not the clear kind, like mine—and really nice green eyes and short brown hair. The braces don't do anything to spoil his cuteness.

Donovan looked around the table. "Okay, I think everyone's here," he said.

Jessica Messina, one of the writers, shook her head. "Beth's not here yet. I'll text her."

"We should get started, anyway," Donovan said. "If we're going to get out an issue out every Friday, then we need to make sure everyone gets their

articles in on time. After I edit them, the design
staff needs to flow them into the layout. We need a
couple of days to get that done. So can everybody
aim for Wednesday?"

Most of us nodded, but Chris raised his hand.
"There's a basketball game on Wednesday I wanted
to cover. Can I get my article to you Thursday
morning?"

Donovan nodded. "One or two late stories are
okay."

"I can get my fashion column to you tonight," I
offered. "I worked on it yesterday."

Donovan said, "That would be great. In fact,
maybe we could move up the deadline for some of
the features to Monday or Tuesday in the future, so
we'll have time to work on the last-minute stuff."

Then Beth Suzuki strolled up to the table. Katie
and I both like Beth a lot. She's really cool, and she
has a very unique sense of fashion besides. Today
she wore plaid pajama pants with a black lace top
over a black tank, and red sneakers. She had spiked
up her short black hair with gel.

"Hey," she said. "I forgot we were meeting today.
I almost got on the bus."

She slid into the seat next to mine, and Donovan
frowned at her.

"Beth, I can start feeding you articles tomorrow," he said. "Do you think we can get your page layouts by Thursday afternoon of this week? Last week we were cutting it a little close."

Beth nodded. "Yeah, Mr. Modica usually lets me do them in computer class, but we had that assembly last week."

Satisfied, Donovan started talking to the other writers about what they were working on. He's good at getting to the point, so the meeting was over pretty soon.

"So, Mia, I wanted to talk to you," Beth said as we stood up.

"Sure," I said. "I've got to wait for my stepdad to pick me up, anyway."

Chris waved good-bye to me, and I waved back as Beth and I made our way out to the hall.

"So, I've been thinking we should start a fashion club," Beth began.

I stopped. "Wow, that's a fabulous idea."

Beth nodded. "Right? I was talking to Libby and Jasmine about it, and they both said we should do it. We could maybe go to fashion shows and talk about fashion and maybe even hold a fashion show ourselves."

My mind started to churn out ideas. We were

just a short train ride away from New York City. (In fact, I take that train every other weekend to see my dad.) We could go on trips, and check out what are in the boutiques, and tour Fashion Avenue, and start a club fashion blog. . . .

"You can join, right?" Beth asked.

I was about to blurt out "Yes!" when I hesitated. The Cupcake Club has an event just about every week. I write a fashion column every week too. I also have soccer at least three nights a week, depending on the season. And then there's the fact I live in another city every other weekend. So I have very little free time, which is why I didn't instantly say yes.

After living in Maple Grove for a while, things had finally started to smooth out. I had a rhythm going. Did I want to add one more thing?

If it was anything else but a fashion club, I probably would have said no. But fashion is my true passion. It's in my blood. I'm even kind of known for it around the school. How could I *not* be in the fashion club?

"Sure, I'll join," I said.

"Cool," Beth said. "We're going to have the first meeting Wednesday after school. Mrs. Carr said we could use the English classroom."

Of course it would have to be Wednesday. The Cupcake Club had started having after-school planning meetings on Wednesdays because it was just about the only day of the week all four of us could be there, at least for a couple of months, anyway.

"Um, I have a Cupcake meeting that day," I said, "but maybe I can miss it."

"Cool," Beth said.

Then a car pulled up in front of the school's entrance, and my stepdad, Eddie, rolled down the window.

"Your limo is here!" he called out. (Eddie is supercorny.) "Does your friend need a ride?"

"My sister's getting me," Beth said, "but thanks."

I climbed into the car.

"Your friend certainly is colorful," Eddie said as we drove off.

"That's Beth," I said. "She's starting a fashion club."

"Well, that's right up your alley," Eddie said. "Sounds like fun."

The more I thought about it, the more excited I got about all the amazing things the fashion club could do. Now I just had to tell the Cupcake Club about it. . . .

CHAPTER 3

A Not-So-Smooth Start

$\mathcal{K}$atie and I take the bus to school together every morning. In fact, that's how we met on the first day of middle school. We still sit in the same seats—six rows from the front—that we sat in the day we met.

We usually talk the whole way to school, and that's normally when I would have told her about stuff like the fashion club. But I felt like I should break it to the Cupcake Club all at once, so I decided to wait.

"So guess what I'm doing this weekend?" Katie asked.

"Um . . . making cupcakes? Reading cupcake cookbooks? Watching cupcake shows on TV?" I teased. Of all of us in the Cupcake Club, Katie is the most cupcake obsessed.

Katie shook her head. "No. Well, maybe one of those things. But mostly Mom wants us to go to the movies with Jeff and Emily."

I raised an eyebrow. Jeff is also known as Mr. Green, a math teacher at our school, and he's dating Katie's mom. It's totally awkward for Katie, and then it got even more awkward when she found out he has a daughter.

"Are you cool with that?" I asked.

Katie shrugged. "I guess. Jeff is always fun to be around, and Emily's really sweet and nice."

"You're lucky she's only a little younger than us and not some little kid," I said, making a face. "Dad says that Lynne and Ethan want to go to the Bronx Zoo this weekend."

"I love the zoo!" Katie said.

"Me too, but Ethan can be such a pain," I complained. "He always has these crying fits, and he's, like, always . . . sticky. It's gross."

Katie laughed. "The other day you were saying how cute he was."

I sighed. "I know. I can't make up my mind."

The bus pulled up to school, and another day of boring classes began. I always look forward to lunch, though, because I get to be with all my friends and we get to catch up. Unfortunately, yesterday I

19

couldn't have lunch with them because I was in the library studying for a Spanish test. So I was really happy to see them all at lunch today.

"Thanks again for texting me those pictures of the craft fair," Emma said as she set down her tray of salad and chicken soup. "I wish I could have been there."

Mom had packed me hummus and vegetables, so after I crunched down on a stick of celery, I said, "We missed you. How did the shoot go?"

"It was fun!" Emma said. "Another catalog. I wore, like, five different pairs of jeans."

You would think because Emma models sometimes she would be a good candidate for the fashion club, but I knew better. She mostly does it to save up money. She has long, blond hair and is really pretty, so I feel like everyone would want to hire her. So far she's done a lot of stuff, and it's always fun when we see her in a catalog or an ad.

Since we were on the topic of modeling, I decided to just come out with the whole fashion club topic.

"So, Beth Suzuki is starting a fashion club," I began.

"That's a great idea," Emma said. "You're joining, right?"

"Yeah," I replied. "Only there's a little problem. The first meeting is tomorrow, and I know we have a Cupcake meeting. I'm so sorry to have to miss it."

"It's okay," Katie said. "I don't think we're planning anything important, right?"

Alexis gave Katie a look. "All of our business is important," she remarked. Then she smiled "But it's probably okay if you're not there. If we need you to brainstorm any decoration ideas, I'll text you."

I felt relieved. "Thanks," I said. "I'll make sure I don't miss any more Cupcake meetings. I just really want to check this out."

"I wish I liked fashion more," Katie said wistfully. "Beth is really nice. I bet you guys will have fun."

It was good to know my friends were okay with my joining the fashion club, and I was kind of excited walking to Mrs. Carr's room after school the next day.

When I got to the room, Beth wasn't there yet. I knew Libby and Jasmine, two girls who Beth hangs out with a lot. Libby has Beth's fashion sense—a little on the punk side, but she's not afraid to mix in wild patterns or add feminine touches, like lace or sequins or pink. She has really straight blond hair that goes down to her shoulders, and there's usually a colored streak in it. This week it was purple.

Jasmine is totally gorgeous—tall and thin with skin the color of caramel and long, braided black hair. She could be a model like Emma if she wanted to. Her style is more like mine—she follows the trends, but keeps it classic, as Mom likes to say, and she adds twists that show off her own personality. Today she had a simple layered look going, with a pale blue tank under a black T-shirt, and she wore these really cool bangle bracelets on both wrists.

There were two other girls there who I didn't really know that well, so I introduced myself after I said hi to Libby and Jasmine.

"Hi, I'm Mia," I said.

"You're in our chorus class," replied one of the girls, who had long, curly brown hair. "I'm Julia, and this is Chelsea."

Chelsea was short, with really big blue eyes in her round face. A hat that looked like a frog's head was perched on top of her choppy brown hair.

"Hey," Chelsea said.

"Oh yeah, we have chorus together," I remembered. "I'm in a fog half the time in there, you know? Mrs. Flores always makes us sing those sappy old songs."

"Chelsea says it's like she's living in the past,"

Julia said with a laugh, and Chelsea smirked next to her.

Libby impatiently tapped a pencil on the table. "So where is Beth, anyway?"

"Here," Beth said, walking into the room, followed by a girl with green eyes and glossy chestnut hair.

I kept myself from groaning out loud. I should have known Olivia Allen would be in the fashion club!

Olivia didn't looked thrilled to see me either.

"Oh, *you're* in this club?" she asked, looking right at me.

I know better than to get into it with Olivia.

"Yes," I replied flatly, and then I sat down at the table.

Olivia and I started out as friends, but she lost my friendship after she was mean to my friends and took advantage of me being a nice person. It's kind of complicated, but it basically meant that we weren't friends anymore. I would have preferred it if she weren't in the club, but I knew she liked fashion as much as I did. That's why we became friends in the first place, so I couldn't really be mad she had joined.

If Beth noticed Olivia giving me a dirty look,

she didn't show it. She sat down at the table.

"So, um, thanks for coming, I guess," she said. "So, I guess we're the Fashion Club."

Julia started clapping and whooping, and I couldn't help laughing. She reminded me of Katie a little bit.

"So, anyway, I had some ideas about what we could do," Beth went on. "Like, maybe we could do a special fashion section for the newspaper. Mia could help with that because she already writes the column."

I nodded. "That's a good idea. We could do a special section for each season, like big newspapers do."

"Can we do a whole section on animal prints?" Julia asked, and that's when I noticed she was wearing a lavender T-shirt with black-and-white zebra stripes across the front, as well as a zebra-striped wristband and zebra-striped socks with her flats.

"I was thinking of doing that for next week's column," I said. "Zebra is trending right now."

"I also thought we could do a fashion show," Beth continued. "You know, like where we get a store to lend us clothes, and we model them and style the other models and everything."

"Oh, I would so love to do that," Jasmine agreed.

"It sounds cool, but I just hope it doesn't take up a lot of time," Libby said, still tapping her pencil. "My mom just doubled up my violin lessons, and now I'm volunteering at the animal shelter on weekends."

Olivia cleared her throat, making it clear she had something important to say.

"Shouldn't we elect officers before we start throwing out ideas?" she asked.

"You mean like president and treasurer and stuff?" Beth asked. "I didn't know if we wanted to do that." Then she turned and looked at me. "Do you have officers in the Cupcake Club?"

"Not exactly," I replied. "We all have different jobs that we do, though."

"It doesn't matter what the *Cupcake Club* does," Olivia interjected, her tone clearly showing what she thought of the club. "This is our club, and we make the rules. And I think we should have officers, like we do in the BFC."

BFC stands for "Best Friends Club," and it's basically made up of the popular girls in our grade. I had no idea they had officers, but I guessed Callie Wilson must be the president,

25

because she's the most popular of all the members.

"Well, I guess . . ." Beth's voice trailed off, and I could tell she didn't really care.

"It's the best way to do it," Olivia pressed on, "so nobody is confused about who's in charge."

Chelsea spoke up for the first time. "Why does somebody have to be in charge?"

"Somebody has to be in charge of when and where we have the meetings, and if we do events, they have to give everybody jobs and stuff," Olivia pointed out.

"If we're going to vote, can we just do it?" Libby asked. "I've got a ton of homework tonight."

"Fine, then let's vote or whatever," Beth said.

"I was president of the dance committee at my old school," Olivia declared, and it was clear what she was hinting at—she wanted to be president of the Fashion Club, too.

It was kind of fun just sitting back and seeing how everything would work out. No way did I want to be in a club if Olivia was president. But I had a feeling I didn't need to speak up.

And I didn't. Libby spoke up right away.

"Beth should be president. This was her idea," Libby said.

"Libby is right," agreed Jasmine.

"Beth should definitely be president," Julia added.

Chelsea shrugged. "Whatever."

That's when I stepped in.

"So, it's settled, then," I said. "Beth is president by a landslide. Congratulations, Beth!"

"But we're supposed to . . . I mean . . ." Olivia was flustered, I could tell.

"I guess we need a vice president, then," Beth said. "Libby, you should do it."

Libby shook her head. "No way. Too busy."

I decided to play nice. I definitely didn't want the job, and Olivia really seemed motivated. "How about Olivia?" I suggested.

Everybody just kind of shrugged.

"Sure."

"Yeah."

"Whatever."

Olivia brightened a little bit after that, and for a second I almost regretted bringing up her name. Olivia with a little power could be a dangerous thing. But it was just a fashion club, after all. I mean, what could she really do?

"Thanks," Olivia said. "Now we need to elect other officers—secretary and treasurer."

"Jasmine's good at math. Jasmine, you should be treasurer," Beth said.

"Sure," Jasmine replied.

"So who wants to be secretary?" Olivia asked, looking at Libby.

I didn't offer to do it. Like I said, the Cupcake Club keeps me pretty busy already. But Julia waved her hand. "I'll do it!"

"Cool," Beth said. "So, um, I guess we could, like, figure out what we want to do."

So we talked for a few minutes about our future plans, and I brought up the idea of going into the city. Julia wrote down everything in a zebra-striped notebook with a zebra-striped pen.

"Can we go now?" Libby asked after a while. "I do not want to be up all night doing my social studies homework."

"Yeah, sure," Beth said.

And that was our first Fashion Club meeting. Not much talking, lots of zebra stripes, and a power play by Olivia. Definitely interesting!

CHAPTER 4

Mixed Feelings

I'm usually in a good mood on Fridays—not just because school is out for the weekend, but because every other Friday I go into the city to see my dad. Even though I like living in Maple Grove with my mom; Eddie; and my stepbrother, Dan, I miss my dad a lot during the week.

We have this tradition on most Fridays: After he picks me up from the train station, we go have sushi. Lately we've been going to Omen, my new favorite restaurant. It's really beautiful and peaceful inside, and we always get a table in the back by the waterfall.

That night I ordered a spicy tuna roll and four pieces of salmon sashimi, which is basically thin slices of salmon on top of little mounds of rice.

Part of the reason I love eating sushi is because of the ritual when you eat it. You pour soy sauce into a tiny ceramic bowl, add a little spicy green wasabi paste and mix it up, and then you pick up the sushi with chopsticks and dip it before you eat it.

That's how I do it, anyway. My dad usually gets a big plate of sashimi, with all different kinds of raw fish. He likes to put a little wasabi on top of the fish and then dip it into the soy sauce. Tonight I noticed that he was piling the green paste on top of a piece of hamachi.

"Dad, I know you like things spicy, but are you really going to eat that?" I asked him.

Dad looked up like I had interrupted his thoughts. "What?" He looked down at his plate. "Oh wow, that would not taste good." Then he scraped off the wasabi mound.

I didn't think too much about it. My dad is an architect, and he's always busy with some new project, so I figured he was thinking about business. He looks businesslike all the time too. He's got black hair that is never out of place because he uses just the right amount of hair gel. He wears tailored suits, and then there are his black glasses, which totally add to the professional look.

My phone chimed, and I took it out of my bag

to check it. "I wonder who's texting me," I said.

"*Mija*, you know how I feel about the phone at dinner," Dad scolded. (*Mija* is kind of like his nickname for me. It means "my daughter" in Spanish, and it sounds a lot like my name.)

"Sorry," I said. "It's Ava. She wants to know if we can do something tomorrow, but I've got to tell her we're going to the zoo."

Dad put down his chopsticks. "About that," he said, and he looked uncomfortable. "I need to tell you something."

"What is it?" I asked, feeling a little worried.

He let out a big breath. "It's Lynne and I," he said. "We . . . we broke up."

It took a moment for this to sink in. "So you're not going to see each other anymore?"

Dad shook his head. "No, honey. I'm sorry. It just didn't work out between us."

I thought about this for a minute. Lynne was nice and everything, and I guess I would miss her a little bit. Then there was Ethan. I had already started to think about what it would be like to have him as my brother—and now I would never see him again. It was a little sad, and a lot weird.

"Are you okay?" I asked Dad.

"Don't worry about me, honey," Dad said.

"Are you okay? I know you liked Lynne."

I shrugged. "Whatever. I'm fine," I said. I mean, I liked her, but I didn't really want her to be my stepmother or anything. I liked Eddie right away, but Lynne, well . . . she was fine, but we really didn't have a lot in common. And every time we were together she was running after Ethan, so we never got a chance to talk too much.

I picked up a piece of spicy tuna roll with my chopsticks and popped it into my mouth. The next few minutes were kind of silent and awkward, and then I realized something.

"So can I see Ava tomorrow?" I asked.

"I don't see why not," Dad replied with a little sigh. "What do you want to do?"

The idea came to me immediately. "Well, I just joined this fashion club in school, and we've been talking about coming into the city on some kind of fashion field trip," I told him. "So maybe Ava and I could go see the Costume Institute's exhibit at the Met. I haven't been there in a while."

Ava is my best friend from the city, and she likes fashion as much as I do. I knew the Costume Institute's exhibit would be the perfect place for a field trip. It's in the Metropolitan Museum of Art, right in the center of Manhattan. There are, like, thousands of costumes and accessories in the collection, and at least once a year they put together an exhibit based around a theme.

"There's a new photography exhibit I've been wanting to see," Dad said, smiling a little for the first time since he'd picked me up. "I'll go with you guys, and we can split up."

"Can I text Ava now?" I asked anxiously.

"Okay," Dad said reluctantly. "Just keep it short."

As I guessed, Ava was more than happy to go. After Dad and I got back to the apartment, I spent the night looking at the museum's website to figure out what I wanted to focus on tomorrow. The exhibit theme this time around was punk fashion from the seventies and how it influenced today's fashion. I realized this would also be the perfect topic for a fashion column, which was great. I could finish the article Sunday night and get it to Donovan early.

So I was feeling pretty good as I got ready for bed, until I opened my bag to unpack and the little stuffed purple monster I'd bought at the craft fair fell out. As soon as I saw it, my eyes started to tear up a little. It was supposed to be for Ethan, but now I would never see him again.

It's silly to cry, I told myself. *He was annoying,*

anyway. But I still couldn't help feeling sad.

I tucked the monster into a pocket in my bag. Emma's little brother, Jake, would like it. I could give it to him. But I was still thinking about Ethan when I went to sleep.

I felt better when I woke up the next morning, and Dad was in a good mood too. He had woken up early and gotten us bagels, which don't seem to taste the same if you get them outside New York City. After breakfast, we walked over to Ava's apartment. She was waiting outside for us.

"Mia Face!" she yelled, giving me a hug, and I knew she was as happy to see me as I was to see her.

"How's everything going?" I asked.

"Good," Ava replied. "What's up with you?"

I thought about telling her about Dad and Lynne's breakup, but Dad was standing right there, so that might have been weird.

"Not much," I replied. "Come on, I'm psyched to see the exhibit."

The Met is a pretty short subway ride away, so we got there pretty fast, but once we got there we found a long line for the costume exhibit. My dad told us he was going to check out the photography exhibit. As soon as he left, Ava and I talked a mile a minute about what was happening with all my old friends from the city, and then I told Ava about the Fashion Club.

"That girl Olivia again?" Ava asked, making a face. "Are you sure you want to be in a club with her?"

I shrugged. "I mean, it's just a club. Believe me, I don't plan on getting involved with her in a close way again. So I figure it'll be all right."

Ava looked dubious, but we changed the subject and talked about the exhibit.

"The exhibit will 'highlight the origins of the punk movement and draw direct connections to haute couture and ready-to-wear creations that it has inspired for the past three decades,'" I read out loud from an article I had found on my phone.

"I love haute couture," Ava said. "All those beautiful, fancy runway clothes."

I nodded. "It's, like, made with the best fabrics and with the finest craftsmanship," I said. "It's kind of weird to think of it and punk in the same sentence, since punk is all about ripped fabric and stuff."

We finally got inside, and it was totally worth the wait. There were photos and costumes from punk rock stars from the seventies, and you could see designer dresses from years later that had some of the same elements—black fabric that looked like spiderwebs, or safety pins that looked like jewels on designer gowns.

I took photos like crazy to show to the Fashion Club. I could definitely see how the punk stuff from back in the seventies influenced what some kids wore today—especially Beth and her friends.

"Beth is going to love this," I said, taking a picture of a rocker in a black jacket covered with random rips, safety pins, and metal studs.

"I think I would wear that," Ava said.

"Yeah, you've got the hair for it," I agreed. Ava is half Korean and half Scottish, and she has the most awesome, glossy black hair that's perfectly straight.

We spent a couple of hours looking around at everything when I got a text from Dad: Hungry! U done? Meet me in food court.

I looked at Ava. "Dad wants us to eat now."

Ava frowned a little. "Aw. There's so much more to look at."

"I know," I said. "But maybe I'll come back with the Fashion Club. You could come back with us."

"I just might," Ava replied. "I need to get a look at this Olivia for myself."

I laughed. "She's not *that* bad, really."

Boy, was I wrong!

CHAPTER 5

Trouble in Parent-dise?

𝒲eekends with Dad always go by superfast, especially when I have to bring homework with me, because my teachers love to give lots of it. Katie always jokes that grading homework papers must be their favorite hobby, and sometimes I'm sure she's right. And what's even better is that even though Mom knows I always do my homework at Dad's, she always bugs me about it when I get home.

"So, are you all done with your homework?" Mom asked as we were eating dinner that Sunday night.

"What do you think?" I replied, stabbing a piece of chicken with my fork, which I know is kind of rude but I am so tired of that question, honestly.

"Mia, a yes or no answer, please," Mom said in a tight voice.

I sighed. "Yes. Like I *always* do."

Mom shook her head. "Honestly, it's a simple question. I don't know why you can't just answer me nicely."

"Well, you never ask *Dan* about his homework," I pointed out.

Eddie turned to Dan with a big smile on his face. "Dan, did you do all your homework?"

Dan was shoveling mashed potatoes into his mouth. He swallowed and said, "Got to finish math. No big deal."

"See? Was that so hard?" Mom asked, looking at me.

I ignored her and took a bite of my chicken.

"So," Eddie said, still smiling. Eddie's always the one who likes to make peace in the house when things get tense. He doesn't like drama. "I'm glad you'll be here next week, Mia. My sister, Connie, and her husband, Simón, are coming for a visit and they'd love to meet you."

Mom's face froze. "What do you mean 'next week'?" she asked.

"I thought I told you," Eddie responded. "Remember, we talked about it a while ago?"

"But I didn't think we decided on a date." Mom's voice was getting high-pitched, like it does when she's upset.

"Honey, I'm sorry," Eddie said. "We can talk about this later, okay?"

Mom nodded, but she didn't say anything. Then she started stabbing her chicken with her fork, just like I was doing.

When dinner was over I helped clear the table, and then I retreated to my room. It's totally, like, my sanctuary in the house, and it took about a year to get it just perfect. The walls are pale turquoise, and the furniture is kind of old, but Eddie helped me paint it glossy white with black trim, so it looks really cool. There's a small drafting table—the slanted kind, so I can sit and draw there if I want—although I end up doing most of my sketches in bed, in a sketch pad.

My favorite thing in my room is the closet, which is almost as big as my whole room in the apartment in Manhattan. I can organize my clothes by season and then by color, which is really helpful since Mom gets a lot of free clothes for me from her designer friends.

I unpacked my bag, stuffing almost everything into my white laundry hamper. The last thing

I pulled out was the purple monster. I quickly stuffed it into my school backpack, so I could give it to Emma. I didn't want to have to keep seeing it.

Then I flopped onto my bed and checked the texts on my phone. There are always a bunch from Katie, Emma, and Alexis, but the first one I saw was from Beth.

Next Fashion Club meeting Wed after school. English room.

Rats! Wednesday again, and I knew I had Cupcake Club meetings on Wednesdays for at least the next month. I couldn't miss two CC meetings in a row. That wouldn't be fair to everyone else. But I didn't want to miss the Fashion Club meeting, either.

I texted Beth, making sure not to reply to every-body else.

Could we move the meetings to Tuesday? I can't do Wednesdays.

To my surprise, Beth texted me back right away.

Y not? CU Tuesday.

40

Then seconds later she sent out a text to everyone saying that the meeting had changed. I felt pretty proud of myself for handling that so well. Now I didn't have any conflict between the Cupcake Club and the Fashion Club. Things were going more smoothly than I had hoped.

Then I saw a text from Katie.

Need to tell you about movie nite w Mom and Jeff, she typed.

Stuff 2 tell u 2, I replied, thinking of Dad's breakup. ☹

Oh no! You OK? Katie asked.

I was about to type a reply when I heard some loud noises outside my room. It kind of sounded like Mom yelling, and I hadn't heard that since I was younger and Mom and Dad got divorced. Curious, I opened my bedroom door.

Mom and Eddie's bedroom door was closed, but the yelling was definitely coming from there. I could make out some of the stuff they were saying.

"You are always making plans without me! What were you thinking?"

"Why is this so upsetting? It's family. You don't plan for family."

"*You* don't plan for family, but *I* do. . . ."

I quickly closed my door. It didn't really matter to me what they were fighting out; what bothered me was that they were fighting.

Mom and Eddie never fought. I mean, never. If anything, they were always kind of lovey-dovey, which was gross, but they never yelled at each other.

I sat on my bed, my mind spinning. Mom and Dad had gotten divorced. Dad and Lynne had broken up. What if Mom and Eddie got divorced next?

This thought scared me a lot more than Dad's breakup, because this was way different. Eddie will never take the place of my dad, but I love him like a dad. And Dan is really cool for a stepbrother, and I've known him a lot longer than I've known Ethan, and I live in the same house with him.

If Mom and Eddie got divorced, we'd have to move out of the house. Would we leave Maple Grove? Go back to Manhattan or to some other place I didn't know? And since Eddie wasn't my real dad, I'd probably never get to see him again.

I didn't cry, but I started to kind of breathe really fast, and my face felt flushed. I tried to calm down; it was just one argument, right? People argue all the time.

But that's how it started with Mom and Dad,

and then there were more and more arguments that got louder and louder.

I wiped the thought from my mind. Mom and Eddie were really happy. *There is nothing to worry about,* I told myself.

But when I went to sleep, it was still on my mind.

CHAPTER 6

Fashion Frustration

*Y*ou never told me about your sad face," Katie said as she slid into the seat next to me on the bus the next day.

"Sad face?" I asked, but then I remembered as soon as I said it. I had never replied to Katie's text the night before. "Oh yeah, that. Well . . . Dad and Lynne broke up."

"No way!" Katie cried. "Seriously? They were dating for a while. What happened?"

I shrugged. "Dad said it just didn't work out or something."

"So, no more Ethan then, I guess?" Katie asked. "That's a good thing, right?"

"Maybe," I said. "I'm not sure. I kind of miss him in a weird way."

Katie looked thoughtful. "I don't know how I would feel if Mom and Jeff broke up. I guess I've kind of gotten used to him. I'd probably miss him and Emily, too."

Of all my friends, I knew Katie would understand. She always does. That's why she's my BFF here.

"So, how did the whole movie date go?" I asked her.

"Pretty good," Katie informed me. "The best part was that Jeff let me and Emily pick out candy from the snack stand, and Mom never lets me get that. She says it's too expensive and rots your teeth. But when Jeff offered to do it, she didn't say *anything*."

"Wow, she must really like him," I said, and then for a second I thought about Mom and Eddie. They used to agree with each other all the time too. But I didn't say anything about that to Katie, because I didn't really feel like talking about it.

At lunch I broke the news about Dad and Lynne to Alexis and Emma, and I gave Emma the little purple monster.

"It was for Ethan, but I thought Jake might like it," I said.

"He'll love it," Emma said. "That's sweet of you."

And then for the first time in days, I felt relieved. I didn't have to talk about the whole thing anymore if I didn't want to—and I really didn't want to.

The next day after school was our next Fashion Club meeting. All the same girls were there, and Beth was late again. I figured out she's one of those people who are always late; people like that are just born that way, I think.

Anyway, as soon as Beth walked in, Olivia started complaining.

"So why are we meeting on Tuesday, exactly?" she asked.

"Mia asked," Beth replied as she took her seat.

Olivia rolled her eyes. "I should have known. Of course we have to change everything around for Mia."

Don't let her get to you. Don't let her get to you, I told myself. Out loud, I said, "If Wednesdays are better for everybody, that's okay with me. I just can't come to every meeting, that's all."

Everyone just kind of shrugged.

"Tuesdays are okay with me," Julia said, and the others nodded in agreement—except for Olivia, of course. But she didn't protest, either.

"Okay, then," Beth said. "So, um, what should we talk about?"

"I did a little research this weekend," I offered. "The Met is doing a costume exhibit, and my friend Ava and I went. It might make a good field trip for us. I took a bunch of photos if you want to see. The theme was punk rock's influence on fashion."

"I read about that," Libby said, looking up from her phone. "We should definitely go."

"Um, I thought we were going to talk about putting on a fashion show," Olivia piped loudly. Everyone looked at her, and she paused for a moment and then smiled. Olivia has this way of getting everyone's attention when she talks; Eddie says people like that have "charisma."

"Oh, right," Beth agreed. "Why? Did you have some ideas?"

"Lots," Olivia said smugly. "At my old school, we had a fashion show, and we got one of the shops in the mall to lend us the clothes. We could probably do the same thing."

"Wait, then who models the clothes?" asked Chelsea. Today she was wearing a hat that looked like a fuzzy bear's head.

"We do, of course," Olivia replied.

Chelsea frowned. "I thought this was a fashion club, not a model club."

"I'll model," Julia volunteered.

"Me too," offered Jasmine.

"Maybe not everyone has to model," I suggested. "We could always get other people to be models, too. And there are lots of other jobs involved in a fashion show, like styling the models and doing the music and organizing things backstage."

"Wow, you're like a fashion show expert," Julia quipped, and I could see Olivia immediately become annoyed.

"My mom is a professional fashion stylist," I said, "so I've been to a lot of shows."

"Well, *of course* not everyone has to model," Olivia chimed in. "Chelsea can do whatever she wants."

"Your mom is a stylist?" asked Chelsea. "That is the coolest thing ever."

"As I was saying," said Olivia, not wanting to lose the spotlight.

"I really like this idea," Beth said. "We could do it on a weekend, in the auditorium."

"I need to check my schedule," Libby said, her eyes glued to her phone again. "I'm pretty sure I've got a violin recital coming up."

Beth nodded. "So I guess we, um, have to make plans and pick jobs and stuff."

"You know, we could get cupcakes from the

Cupcake Club for the event," I suggested. "People always want to eat something at a fashion show."

"You mean, like, we should buy cupcakes to give away for free?" Olivia asked with another classic eye roll. "First of all, we don't have a budget. Second, fashion shows usually have grapes and cheese and stuff like that. Cupcakes are so juvenile."

"We have provided cupcakes for a fashion show before," I said defensively. "We do all kinds of events."

At this point, I couldn't help noticing that Beth was being pretty wishy-washy about everything we talked about. Wasn't she supposed to be the club president? Olivia kept putting down everything I had brought up, and it would have been nice to get a little support from Beth.

"We probably shouldn't worry about refreshments just yet," Libby remarked. "Shouldn't we, like, figure out what kind of clothes we want for the show?"

"We could go to the mall," Olivia said. "Friday night?"

I looked at the calendar on my phone. On Friday I had typed in "CC baking night."

"I can't go Friday," I said.

Olivia looked around. "Can everyone else go?"

"I can go at seven," Libby replied as everyone else nodded. "Is that okay?"

"Perfect," Olivia said. "Sorry you can't go, Mia. Maybe the Fashion Club is too much for you, with your busy schedule and all."

"No, it's fine," I snapped. Olivia was starting to get under my skin, and I hated that.

"Then it's settled, then," Olivia said, looking very pleased with herself.

I was starting to think I had made a big mistake in joining the club when Libby surprised me.

"Hey, can we look at those photos you took at the punk exhibit?" she asked.

"Yeah, I'd like to see them too," Chelsea added.

"Sure," I replied, reaching into my backpack. I had printed them out at home and made a quick presentation out of them. Everybody gathered around to look at them and seemed pretty excited about planning a trip, even Olivia. So that was nice, and I decided to stick with the Fashion Club. I wasn't going to let Olivia spoil it for me.

I just hoped Olivia wouldn't spoil it for everyone else, too.

CHAPTER 7

Cupcake Confidential

That night at dinner I reminded Mom and Eddie about my weekend schedule.

"Friday is cupcake baking, and Katie's mom said I could sleep over," I reported. "Saturday morning is cupcake delivery, and then I've got soccer practice Sunday morning. But I'll be around Saturday night for dinner, Eddie. We're having dinner with Connie and Simón, right?"

"Oh, that," Eddie said, suddenly looking uncomfortable. "We're not doing that on Saturday after all."

I looked at Mom, but she was staring down at her bowl of pasta. I guess she had won that argument. So it was over, but things seemed to be a little tense between her and Eddie, and I started to worry again. First, Dad and Lynne, and now maybe Mom and Eddie?

Maybe it was my imagination, but Mom and Eddie seemed to be less lovey-dovey all week, too. By the time Friday night's cupcake baking came around, I was starting to freak out again. It's a good thing I had a sleepover with Katie.

Before the sleepover we had a baking session. Emma, Alexis, and I got to Katie's house in time for dinner, because Katie's mom had made her famous chili for us. Then we got down to baking.

"First, we should do the mini cupcakes for The Special Day," Alexis said, looking up from her clipboard. "Then we need to make two dozen lemon cupcakes for the baby shower, and those should be pretty easy too."

We have a long-standing order to make mini cupcakes for the bridal salon in town, The Special Day. They do a little fashion show of the new dress styles, and they serve the cupcakes as refreshments. It's an easy job, and Mona, the owner of the shop, lets us put out business cards, so sometimes we get clients from it.

"I can do the mini cupcakes delivery tomorrow, because Mona asked me to model bridesmaids dresses," Emma said.

"You are so going to be a famous model some-day," Katie remarked. "Promise you won't forget me when you're famous!"

Emma made a face. "I'm not so sure if I want to do it forever. But it is kind of fun now."

"There's a girl in the Fashion Club who looks just like a model," I said. "Do you guys know Jasmine?"

Emma nodded. "She hangs out with Libby and Beth, right? She should model. I can tell Mona about her. Maybe she could sub for me on the days I can't do it."

"I'll tell her," I said "Thanks."

"So how is the Fashion Club going?" Alexis asked, and I knew she was dying for dirt about Olivia. Fortunately I was in the mood to dish.

"Olivia is being really bossy about everything," I reported. "Beth is the president of the club, but at the last meeting, Olivia tried to run everything. We're trying to plan a fashion show, and it's like she won't listen to anyone else's ideas. Like, I suggested they could get cupcakes from us for refreshments, and Olivia shot that down fast."

"Why?" Alexis asked.

"Well, first she said we didn't have a budget," I answered. "But then she said cupcakes were too *juvenile* for a fashion show. Can you imagine?"

Emma shook her head. "That's ridiculous!"

"She has a point about the budget," Alexis said reasonably. "I mean, you guys just started. But she's just being mean about the second part."

"I know," I agreed.

Alexis thought for a minute. "You know, we could donate some cupcakes for the fashion show," she said. "It's a nice thing to do for a fellow club, and it's good publicity."

"Really? That would be so cool!" I said. I looked at Emma and Katie. "Are you guys okay with it?"

"Of course!" Katie said, and Emma nodded.

"We can pay for the ingredients out of our publicity budget," Alexis said, furiously scribbling on the pad on her clipboard. "How many people do you think will attend?"

"Um, I'm not sure," I admitted.

"Okay. So how are you guys publicizing it?" Alexis asked. "If you're doing posters or programs, you could put us down as a sponsor. That's free advertising."

"We didn't really discuss that yet," I said kind of sheepishly.

Alexis made that little *tsk-tsk* sound. "Fine. Can you just tell me the date and where it is?"

Now I felt really silly. "Um . . ."

"Just get back to me when you get more details, and I'll put it on the schedule," Alexis said matter-of-factly. "Okay, let's get baking!"

Katie made the batter for the mini cupcakes, Alexis prepared the pans, Emma made the icing, and I got started on the flower decorations for the baby shower cupcakes. They were pretty simple, but I still needed time to do them right.

I took some pale-yellow fondant and rolled it out into a thin sheet. Then I used a tiny flower-shape cookie cutter to cut little flowers out of the fondant. We had to deliver two dozen cupcakes, but I cut out thirty flowers, just in case some of them got messed up. The last step was to use a paintbrush (one I used just for food) to paint little orange centers in each flower with food coloring.

Emma looked over my shoulder. "So pretty!"

"Thanks," I said. "They're pretty simple, but it works."

"The mini cupcakes are cool if you want to frost those, Mia," Alexis said. "I'm going to start the lemon batter."

Even though we all take turns doing jobs, some of us are better at different stuff. Katie and Emma are really good at coming up with recipes. Alexis is a pro at organizing our whole business, but she can also whip up a superfluffy frosting every time. And because I'm artistic, I usually am the one to make decorations and apply the frosting.

I used a tiny spatula to carefully apply the white frosting onto the mini cupcakes. The spatula is a great tool because it lets you get the frosting nice and smooth. Sometimes we use a pastry bag to squirt the frosting on top, but Mona wants neat cupcakes so nothing gets on the clothes.

"I don't know how you do it, Mia," Katie said, looking over at me. "I can never get it smooth."

"I don't know; I just can," I replied.

"She's got a steady hand," Alexis said, cracking an egg into the batter.

I looked back to the cupcakes, carefully smoothing the icing over each one. It felt kind of relaxing, and it's supersatisfying to see the tiny, perfect cupcakes when you're all done. I carefully placed them into a cardboard bakery box and then sealed it with a sticker that had our logo on it.

By the time we finished everything, including cleaning the kitchen, it was nine o'clock. Alexis's dad came to pick up her and Emma, and Katie and I went upstairs to her room.

Katie's room is a lot like her personality—really

colorful. I flopped down on a purple beanbag chair, and Katie got on the floor and hugged a rainbow-shape pillow. She always says "rainbow" is her favorite color, even though it's not really one color.

"Yay! Sleepover!" Katie said. "Mom said we could stay up late and watch a movie if we want. But we have to start it by ten."

"Nothing scary," I said.

Katie shivered. "You know I don't like scary movies," she said. "I was thinking we'd watch the one about the girls who form a band."

I nodded. "Awesome," I said, and then I guess I sighed. Now that we were done with cupcakes, all my worries about Mom and Eddie came back.

"You okay?" Katie asked.

"Yeah," I replied. "It's just . . . you know how I told you about Dad and Lynne breaking up?"

Katie nodded.

"Well, now Mom and Eddie are fighting," I said. "I mean, they had one fight, but they still seem kind of mad at each other, and I'm worried. It reminds me of what happened before my mom and dad got divorced."

"That had to be awful," Katie said sympathetically.

"I guess you were a baby when your parents got

divorced, right?" I asked. "So you wouldn't remember if they were fighting or not."

Katie shook her head. "You know, I don't even remember living with my dad," she confessed, and she turned away for a second. Recently there's been this whole drama with Katie's dad trying to get back into her life, and she's just not into it yet. But I know she thinks about it a lot.

"I did look up a bunch of stuff on the Internet about divorce," Katie admitted. "Just to try and figure out what happened, because Mom doesn't like to talk about it. She did tell me that things were stressful because Dad was trying to figure out what to do with his life. Then I read that stress in the house is, like, a leading cause of divorce. But your house isn't stressful."

I thought about that. "I don't think so," I said cautiously. "But Dan and I do argue about stuff sometimes. And my mom gets upset when I forget to wear my glasses when I'm supposed to. And Eddie gets annoyed when I take milk out of the fridge for my cereal and then forget to put it back."

Suddenly I could think of a hundred things I've done that might cause stress in the house.

"Oh no." I groaned. "What if *I'm* the source of the stress?"

"No way!" Katie said. "That stuff you do is all normal stuff everyone does. Don't be silly."

I sighed. "I can't help it. I'm just really worried."

"You said it was just one argument, right?" Katie asked. "It's probably nothing."

"I hope so," I said.

"Hey, let's go watch the movie," Katie said, and then she wiggled her eyebrows. "Don't forget your glasses, okay?"

I picked up a pillow and smacked her knees with it. "Very funny . . . *Mom!*"

That's another reason I love Katie: She can always put me in a good mood!

CHAPTER 8

Compromising Isn't Easy!

$\mathcal{K}$atie and I delivered the cupcakes for the baby shower on Saturday, and then I spent the afternoon doing homework till Mom knocked on my door.

"Put on something nice," she said. "We're going out to dinner."

"With who?" I asked.

"Eddie's sister," Mom replied, and then she closed the door before I could ask any more questions.

I put on some black skinny jeans, a blue knit top, and a black boyfriend blazer, and pulled on my favorite short black boots. I slipped on a light blue infinity scarf with little black xs all over it, just for fun. Then I went downstairs.

Mom and Eddie were dressed up and getting

ready to go. Mom kept smoothing her dress, as though she was a little nervous.

"Where's Dan?" I asked.

"Working at the ShackBurger," Eddie said. "He's going to visit with his aunt tomorrow. But I'm glad you're going to meet Connie after all." Then he smiled at Mom.

Mom didn't smile back. "Let's go," she said.

We ended up driving out of Maple Grove, all the way to a Spanish restaurant in Hudson City. It started to rain a little, and Mom and Eddie weren't talking much, so I put in my earbuds and listened to music while I went online on my phone, looking at fashion websites. I'm glad I had all that stuff with me because there was a lot of traffic, and it took forever to get there. It was kind of weird that I had never met Connie before, but she and Simón lived in another country and had just moved back here about a month ago. Eddie and Mom had picked her up at the airport, but I was at my dad's that weekend.

The dinner was good and everything, and Eddie's sister and her husband were nice, but it was kind of boring because I was the only kid with four adults. Nobody really talked to me except to ask typical questions like, "How do you like school?"

One of these times I'm going to give Katie's favorite answer: Closed. And I'm not allowed to go on my phone when we're out to dinner so I just had to sit there and eat.

As soon as we got back in the car I turned on my phone again.

"There's going to be so much traffic on the way home," Mom said with a sigh.

"Well, it would have been much easier if we had just—" Eddie began.

"Oh please," Mom said. "I thought this was all settled. We had a nice night, didn't we?"

I put in my earbuds again, feeling more worried than before. I did not like this at all.

I couldn't stop thinking that I was part of the stress that was making Mom and Eddie fight. So the next day I went out of my way to be a perfect child. After breakfast, I cleared the whole table without being asked. After soccer practice, I put my dirty clothes in the laundry, ran the machine, and then took the clothes out of the dryer and folded them.

As I was putting a pile of towels into the linen closet, Mom walked up and hugged me.

"You're being so helpful today, Mia. Thank you!" she said, hugging me.

Then Eddie walked into the hall. "Mia is always

sweet and helpful. She takes after her mother."

Mom smiled and turned around and hugged Eddie, and I smiled too. My plan was working!

So I was in a pretty good mood for the next couple of days, up until the Fashion Club meeting on Tuesday. Then I wasn't exactly in a bad mood—just an Olivia mood.

When the meeting started, Olivia started talking right away, like she was the president. Beth didn't seem to mind, though. I was starting to think she was the most laid-back person I had ever met.

"Our Friday trip to the mall was a success," Olivia announced. "Trendz is going to lend us clothes for our fashion show!"

"Trendz?" I asked, and I know I was frowning. Trendz is this new store that opened up, and the clothes are kind of flashy. I mean, I know everyone's sense of style is different, but I don't even think you could call the clothes at Trendz stylish. It is definitely not my favorite store.

"Yes, Trendz," Olivia repeated. "Isn't that awesome?"

"That girl who works there was really nice," Julia said. "What was her name?"

"Nikki," Beth answered. "Yeah, she was really cool."

Then I remembered I had good news for the club. "Guess what? I talked to my friends in the Cupcake Club, and we're going to provide free cupcakes for the show. So it won't cost us anything, and our guests will get free refreshments."

Olivia frowned. "Cupcakes and fashion do not mix."

"But I like cupcakes," Julia protested.

"Yeah, and they're free," added Chelsea.

"I think it's nice," Beth commented. "Thanks, Mia."

"No problem," I said. "Once we decide on a theme for the show, we can make cupcakes to match the theme."

"What do you mean a theme?" Olivia asked.

"Well, most fashion shows have a theme," I said. "Sometimes it's for a season, or, like, a prom fashion show or something. But a lot of the designers have artistic themes."

"Ooh, yeah, they always do themes on that *Project Design* show," Julia said. "This one designer did 'Mystical Winter,' and the dresses were all white and silvery."

I nodded. "Yeah. Like that."

"We should pick a theme when we pick out what clothes we're going to wear," Libby suggested.

"Nikki said we could pick them out next weekend, right?"

"Right," Beth said.

"We should go Friday again," Olivia said quickly.

Of course she would say that, when I was going to be with my dad Friday night. She probably remembered it from when we were friends.

"Um, I go to my dad's every other weekend," I said. "But sometimes I get home early on Sunday. Could we go Sunday afternoon?"

Guess what Olivia did next? She rolled her eyes, of course. "Mia, your schedule is even worse than Libby's," she complained.

"Actually, Friday night is bad for me too," Libby said. "Sunday works."

Jasmine, Beth, Julia, and Chelsea also agreed to Sunday at two o'clock, and I was relieved.

"I'll meet you guys there," I promised. "My mom can drop me off after she picks me up at the train station."

"Cool," Beth said. "Then I guess we're good."

"Um, did we decide on a date for the show yet?" I asked, thinking of everything Alexis had brought up on Friday night. "And a time? And we should probably talk about doing posters and programs and stuff."

"I was thinking we could do the sixteenth," Beth said. "That's a Saturday. And maybe we could do, like, seven o'clock? How does that sound?"

Nobody had a problem with the date, not even Libby, so that got settled quickly.

"I'll do posters," Beth offered.

Jasmine raised her hand. "And I can do the program."

Wow, this is easy, I thought. Alexis had made it seem so complicated.

"Okay, then, so I guess we'll met at Trendz on Sunday," Beth said. "Thanks."

Just like before, the Fashion Club meeting had started out rough (thanks to Olivia) and then smoothed out at the end. My English teacher would say, "All's well that ends well." Except things were really just beginning.

CHAPTER 9

Friendz and Trendz

$\mathcal{H}$ow was your weekend with Dad?" Mom asked when I climbed into the passenger seat on Sunday.

"Good," I told her. "We walked around Fashion Avenue, and I took some pictures to show to the Fashion Club. I guess I can use them for my newspaper column, too, so that's good. How was your weekend?"

"Very nice," Mom said, smiling, and I felt relieved, but I wasn't taking any chances.

"Are you sure it's not any trouble to drop me off at the mall?" I asked.

"Not at all," Mom replied. "Actually, I'm going to go in, because I need to do some shopping. Text me when you're ready to go, okay?"

"Okay," I said and then added, "When I get home, I'll vacuum my room."

Mom looked at me curiously. "That would be great, Mia. Thanks for thinking of it."

Sunday is a busy day at the mall, but we lucked out and found a parking spot by the Taste of Italy entrance. Once we got inside I stopped at the directory and found Trendz right above us on the second floor, so I said good-bye to Mom and took the escalator up a flight.

I actually heard Trendz before I saw it, because deafening pop music blared from the speakers outside. Inside, hot pink lights flashed on and off, illuminating the clothing displays.

I found the Fashion Club girls at the counter, talking to a girl who looked a little older than a high schooler. She had long, curly auburn hair, and she wore this cute little striped beanie on top of her head. I thought her bright pink lipstick looked pretty cool, and she wore a really long silver necklace with her gauzy white top. I figured this was the Nikki they had talked about at the meeting.

"Hi, Mia!" Julia called out, waving as I walked in. I smiled when I saw her.

"Hi!" I replied, running up to the counter. "Hope I'm not late."

"No," Beth said. "Nikki was just telling us what to do."

Nikki smiled. "Hey. So I was just saying you can pick out a total of twelve outfits and leave them here until the day of the fashion show. My manager said it's okay, but we just need to log everything in."

Julia raised her hand. "Do you have zebra stripes?" she asked. She happened to be wearing zebra leggings and a black T-shirt, with a zebra headband in her hair.

Nikki laughed. "Lots. Go ahead and look around."

Julia ran straight for a rack of animal print clothes, and everyone started to walk around, looking. Like I mentioned before, this isn't exactly my favorite store in the mall, although to be fair, I hadn't really explored it much. The loud music and pink lights were kind of a turnoff. But Nikki looked cool, and salespeople usually wear clothes from the store they work in, so I had hope.

I was rummaging through a rack of too-short skirts when Olivia came up next to me. She pulled out a neon yellow skirt and held it up to her waist. It came down about six inches above her knees.

"This would look amazing with that fuschia blazer over there, wouldn't it?" she asked.

Now, Olivia does have amazing fashion sense, but I think she was off on this one. "I don't know. It's a little short, isn't it? Maybe if you paired it with leggings?"

Olivia rolled her eyes and walked off. I abandoned the skirts and went to a rack of dresses. There were mostly bright colors and loud prints, and a lot of the dresses had big ruffles in weird places that I didn't love. But then I found something pretty decent: an emerald green party dress with short sleeves and a little collar, and it flared out a little bit from the waist. It was vintage inspired but still really cute, and I started to think of a dozen ways I could accessorize it.

Beth and Libby were looking through the rack next to me, so I held it up to show them.

"This is really nice. What do you guys think?" I asked.

"I totally love that," Beth agreed. "You could pretty it up with heels, or punk it out with boots and it would still look good."

Olivia must have overheard, because she walked right over.

"Oh, Mia, I saw that dress last week," she said, reaching out for it. "I was going to wear that."

I couldn't believe it! No way did I believe that

70

Olivia had claims on that dress. She just wanted it because she saw how awesome it was.

I nodded toward the three dresses she held in her right hand. "Oh really? What about those?"

"Those are for the *other* models we're recruiting," Olivia countered. "We're supposed to be looking for dresses for them, too."

Helplessly, I looked to Beth and Libby. Thankfully, Beth jumped in and saved the day for me, although I don't even think she realized she was doing that.

"What about that flower print dress you found last week, Olivia?" she asked. "I thought that looked gorgeous on you."

Flattered, Olivia blushed a little. "Oh yeah, that one. Do you really think it's nicer than this one?"

"I just remember it looked perfect on you," Beth responded. "You should try it on again."

Olivia nodded and then ran to find the flowered dress.

"Thanks," I said. "I should try this on."

"It's going to look great with your coloring," Libby said, and I gave her a grateful smile.

After that, things were kind of fun. Everyone found an outfit they liked, and we picked out six more outfits for the other models to wear. Julia found a whole crazy look with zebra print leggings and a top. The flower print dress Olivia tried on really did look nice; it was kind of vintage inspired, like mine.

But Olivia got her way and picked some of the really short skirts for the models, and Jasmine loved the dresses with the weird ruffles, so I was a little worried about how awesome our fashion show would ultimately be. *Maybe we can save it with styling,* I thought. Mom says you can save any outfit if it's styled right.

"We should take pictures of everything, so we can think about how to style the outfits," I suggested. "We can also figure out the order of how the outfits come out. You want to start out with something strong and then end with your strongest piece."

"I *love* your dress," Julia gushed. "You should go last."

From the corner of my eye, I saw Olivia scowl. It wasn't my fault I was able to pick out the best dress in the place. It's like she can't stand it unless she gets all the attention for herself!

"I think we should decide the order of the outfits *as a group,*" Olivia said.

72

"Sure. Whatever," Beth agreed. "We can do it at our next meeting."

Olivia looked pleased. "So, hey, we should go to Smoothie Paradise now."

That actually sounded nice. I liked the other girls in the Fashion Club, especially Julia, and it would have been fun to hang out with them. But I was kind of needing an Olivia break.

"My mom's here," I said, taking out my phone. "So I can't stay. Maybe next time."

I quickly texted my mom and told her I was done. To my relief, she was just a few stores away.

"See you Tuesday," I said, waving, and then I headed out to catch up with Mom.

"How did it go?" Mom asked when we found each other.

"Okay," I said. "I don't love that store, but we found some nice stuff."

"I'm sure it'll be great," Mom assured me. "And I'm glad you're done. Eddie's making his famous spaghetti, and he wants us to get home soon."

"Mmm, spaghetti," I said, and I felt great. Every time a little problem cropped up, it worked out just fine. I am a much happier person when things are nice and smooth.

CHAPTER 10

What a Disaster!

$\mathcal{I}$ told my friends about the Trendz incident when we had lunch on Monday.

"Oh my gosh! You mean Olivia actually tried to take the dress you wanted?" Katie asked.

I nodded. "Yeah, but luckily Beth convinced her to wear another dress."

"She sounds like a pretty diplomatic leader," Alexis remarked.

I shrugged. "I guess. I'm not exactly sure if she did it on purpose or not, you know? She just kind of goes with the flow."

"Well, at least everything worked out," Alexis said. "You guys sound like you're a lot more organized than you were before."

"Hey, guys," Emma said, motioning with

her head toward Beth, who was walking right toward us.

"Hey," Beth greeted us, nodding as she came up to the table. "Mia, I wanted to show you the posters I made. I worked on them all last night, practically."

"Cool," I said, and Katie scooted into an empty seat so that Beth could sit between us. She had a small cardboard box that held what looked like a hundred flyers.

"I used up, like, two color cartridges printing them out," Beth said. "What do you think?"

"They're gorgeous!" I exclaimed, and I meant it. Her design was bold and really, well, fashiony at the same time. The main feature was this sort of abstract ink drawing of a girl in a dress, and Beth had accented everything in purple and turquoise, which was really attention-getting. She even added a nice mention of the Cupcake Club, thanking us for donating cupcakes.

"I love the colors," Katie added, looking over Beth's shoulder at the poster.

"Did you do the illustration?" I asked Beth.

She nodded. "Yeah, is it okay?"

"It's really chic," Emma said from behind me. "You're an awesome artist."

Beth blushed a little. "Thanks."

Alexis held out her hand. "Can I see? I want to get the date and time into my calendar."

I passed her one across the table, and after she studied it for a minute she frowned.

"That's weird," she said. "I'm pretty sure the chess club has the auditorium that night."

"The chess club?" I asked.

"I think they reserved the auditorium for a chess tournament," Alexis explained. "Did you guys get the date approved in the office?"

I was starting to get a bad feeling about everything. Beth looked kind of confused.

"What do you mean?" Beth asked.

"Well, you can't just say you're going to do something in the auditorium without checking with the office first," Alexis explained patiently. "First, they make sure the date is free, and then they have to approve the event. So I'm guessing you didn't do that?"

Beth shook her head.

Alexis typed into her smartphone. "See? The date's taken," she said, holding up the phone so we could see. "So is every date for the next five weeks."

"Oh man, that stinks," Beth said, and I couldn't believe how calm she sounded. "After I made all these posters and everything."

What a disaster! I thought. But I didn't say it, because I didn't want to upset Beth.

"So, what do we do?" I worried out loud. "Do we cancel the show?"

"You'll have to find another venue, unless you want to put it off for five weeks," Alexis informed us. She looked at her phone again and shook her head, frowning.

"Maybe we can find another place," I said, thinking. "I could ask my mom about the Women's Club's space."

"That would be cool," Beth said. Then she looked down at the posters. "Printing out new posters is going to stink, though. Those ink cartridges are expensive."

I took another look at the poster. "Well, if we just change the place, we could just print out this one line to save paper and ink, and then cut it out and glue it on."

Beth nodded. "That would be cool. Just let me know what your mom says."

"I'm surprised Mrs. Carr didn't tell you about reserving the auditorium," Alexis remarked. "Isn't she your adviser?"

"She said we could meet in her room, but I don't know," Beth said. "I didn't think we needed a teacher telling us what to do, you know?"

She glanced at me. "Talk to you soon," she said, and then she packed up the box and walked back to her table. Alexis rolled her eyes as she walked away. I kind of thought that was a little mean on Alexis's part, but I got it. Beth wasn't exactly on top of things; that was obvious. The Fashion Club would be a lot more organized if we had our very own Alexis.

"Well, it sounds like things will work out," Katie said helpfully.

"I hope so," I said, and Alexis gave Emma a look, like a *What is she, kidding?* look. But I ignored that too, because the last thing I needed was stress within the Cupcake Club, since that was the only area of my life going smoothly.

I knew I had to figure out this fashion show problem right away, so when I got home from school, I made sure Mom would be in a good mood so I could ask her a favor. I set the dining room table for dinner, and then I did my homework on the kitchen table. That's how Mom found me when she came into the house. Our little white dogs, Tiki and Milkshake, ran to the door, yipping and yapping to greet her.

"Why, hello, Mia," she said. "You're doing your

homework already? How smart of you."

"Yeah, that's me," I said. "I'm smart."

After Mom hung up her coat, she went into the dining room, and a minute later she stuck her head into the kitchen.

"Thank you for setting the dinner table," she said. "Unless that was Dan."

"Right. Because an alien took over Dan's brain," I said. "Of course it was me!"

Mom smiled. "I guess I knew that. You've been doing a lot of nice things lately, Mia."

I shrugged. "It's no big deal. I can help you make dinner if you want. I'm almost done with my math."

"I've got dinner," Mom said, "but thank you."

"Well, if I'm done early, I'll walk Tiki and Milkshake," I promised.

By the time we all sat down to dinner, Mom was looking at me a little suspiciously. I knew she was wondering why I was being such a perfect child. It was kind of a good thing I had already started to do the angelic act a week ago, because now I knew Mom would help me find a new place for the fashion show.

"So, Mia," she said. "How was your day?"

"Well," I said, putting down my fork. "There's

kind of a little problem with the fashion show we're planning. Beth never reserved the auditorium with the office, and now the date is taken. So we were hoping maybe we could have the show in the Women's Club's space?"

"Oh," Mom said, like she was surprised I hadn't revealed something much worse. "I'm sure we could do that. What date is it?"

"The sixteenth," I said.

Mom nodded. "I'll call Mrs. Barrows after dinner."

For the rest of dinner I noticed Mom and Eddie were laughing and joking like normal (and Dan was quietly stuffing his face like normal). So I guessed my perfect child thing had worked, although I figured I should keep it up for a while. I didn't want to take any chances.

Later, I was up in the room when Mom came up to deliver the good news: The Fashion Club could use the Women's Club's space for our fashion show on the sixteenth. I felt really relieved—and I hoped this was the last thing that would go wrong with the fashion show. I didn't need Alexis rolling her eyes at us anymore!

CHAPTER 11

Bold Moves

The next afternoon I was excited to tell everyone in the Fashion Club that my mom had saved the day. So I kind of pulled an Olivia and started talking as soon as the meeting started.

"So, you know how the auditorium was booked by the chess club on the sixteenth?" I began. Beth's friends Libby and Jasmine nodded, but the other girls looked confused—even Olivia.

"But that's the night of *our* fashion show," Olivia protested.

"Well, it still can be the night of our fashion show," I said. "The auditorium is not available, but my mom belongs to the Women's Club in town, and they'll let us use their space for free."

"Woo-hoo!" Julia cheered, clapping, and

Chelsea, Beth, Libby, and Jasmine started clapping too. Olivia folded her arms across her chest.

"Shouldn't we have talked this over as a group?" Olivia asked. "Or are you, like, taking over the whole fashion show?"

I was kind of shocked Olivia would say that. "No, I was just trying to help, that's all," I protested, and then I felt a little angry. "You know, if my friend Alexis hadn't seen the poster, we might never have found out about the mistake. It could have been a total disaster." I felt a little bad saying that, but Beth had messed up pretty big, and my mom had totally saved the day.

Olivia looked down at her notebook.

"Anyway, it's all good now," Beth said.

"Maybe we should go visit the space, so we know how to, like, set it up," Libby suggested.

I nodded. "That's a good idea. I'll ask my mom. But in the meantime I think they have photos on their website we can look at."

"Before we do that, we need to think of a theme for the show," Olivia said. Which was a good idea, as I had mentioned before, but I was starting to hate how Olivia had to disagree with everything I said.

Olivia took a poster board from her backpack

that was covered with printed-out pictures of dresses and outfits.

"This is the stuff we picked out on Sunday," she said. "I thought I would make a display so we can see what we're dealing with. I had some theme ideas. How about, 'Saturday Night Fever'?"

"Isn't that some old movie?" Julia asked.

"Well, yes, but that's not the point," Olivia replied. "It's, like, these are all clothes you could wear on a Saturday night, and the 'fever' is because they make you look hot."

"That was a disco movie," Chelsea said in a tone that showed she clearly did not like disco. "I will not be in a show named after a disco movie."

Olivia frowned. "Okay, how about this one: 'Fun and Flirty'?"

"That's a cute title, but I don't think these clothes are flirty," Libby said. "When I think of flirty, I think of pale colors and flowers and stuff. But these colors are more bold."

Olivia looked totally frustrated. "But—"

"'Bold' is a really good word," Julia interrupted. "Maybe the theme could be 'Bold' . . . 'Bold and . . .'"

"'Beautiful'?" Jasmine asked. "Oh wait, isn't that a TV show?"

"How about 'Bold Moves'?" I suggested.

"Hey, I like that," Beth said. "Then we could go with really bold music and decorations and stuff."

"Yeah, like seventies glam rock or something, or maybe even metal," Chelsea said, nodding. "I can work on a playlist."

"And we can do zebra decorations!" Julia cried.

"Or we could pick some of the bold colors that stand out from the outfits we've picked, and use some of those," I suggested, "so that the decorations don't distract from the clothes."

Beth pointed to Olivia's display. "When I was doing the poster, I picked purple and turquoise because those colors popped from the photos we took," she said. "What about those?"

"I like it," Chelsea said.

"Could we please have one little zebra balloon?" Julia asked.

We all laughed. "Definitely," Beth said. "But just one."

I was starting to feel excited. We had a date, a place, the clothes, and we had ideas for music and decorations. Oh, and cupcakes! While the girls talked about friends they had who could model, I pulled out a sketch pad and started to work on cupcake designs. Bold . . . bold . . . We could dye the icing purple and turquoise. That could be cool. Or should we go with bold flavors instead? I had been wanting to make a dark chocolate cupcake with a kick of jalapeño, but the right event hadn't come up yet.

I kind of got lost in my sketching, and then I heard Olivia say, "So we've got our model list finalized."

I put down my pencil. "Sorry. The list is all done? 'Cause I was thinking I could ask Emma. She's, like, a professional."

"*Sorry*, but it's all filled up," Olivia said. "We're all modeling except for Chelsea, and I'm getting Callie, Bella, and Maggie, and Julia's cousin Mikayla is going to do it, and Beth already asked Lucy and Sophie. Twelve outfits, twelve models."

Callie, Bella, and Maggie were all in the BFF club with Olivia. I should have known they would get involved somehow. I hoped Emma wouldn't be hurt that I didn't ask her, but there was nothing I could do.

Libby looked at her phone. "Are we done yet? I have to get to practice."

"I guess," Beth said. "Although, it would be good to get the posters done so we can start putting them up."

85

She held up a flash drive and looked at me. "I brought the file with me so we can cut and paste that one line, print it out, and then glue it on the poster, like you said."

"Do you think we can use the computer room to print it out?" I asked.

Beth shrugged. "We can check."

As Beth and I were talking, everybody else was getting their stuff together and leaving.

"This will go fast if we all help," I said, but everybody just kept talking and heading out the door.

"Let's check out the computer room," I said with a sigh.

We got lucky—I guess. Mr. Modica, the computer teacher, was still there, and he said we could use the computer and printer since it was for a school club. Beth made a file with the new location of the fashion show so that it fit on one line, and she did it so that the line repeated fifteen times on one sheet of paper. This way we only had to print seven color pages instead of a hundred.

Then we went to the art room, and we used a paper cutter to cut the lines into strips. We sat at one of the tables and used glue sticks to attach on the new lines.

While we were working, Eddie texted me.

Your meeting done yet?

I looked at the stack of posters in front of me.

Give me 1/2 hour, I texted back.

The time went fast because Beth and I talked about stuff, but by the time we were done and I got home, it was already dinnertime. I had a ton of homework, so I really didn't want to do the perfect child thing and clear the table and stuff, but I didn't want to jinx anything, so I kind of rushed through it. Then I finally got to start my homework, and I had to finish this huge lab report for Ms. Chandar in science and it took forever.

By the time I was done, I was so tired that I fell asleep really fast. When I woke up I was still so tired that Mom had to pull the covers off me. Maybe things were finally working out with the Fashion Club, but it sure was a lot of work!

CHAPTER 12

I Really Mess Up!

So the Fashion Club has decided on a theme for our show," I told my friends the next day at lunch. "It's 'Bold Moves.'"

"That sounds exciting," Katie remarked. "So are you using bold colors?"

I nodded. "We're focusing on purple and turquoise."

"Ooh, turquoise cupcakes," Emma said. "I can just picture them. That could be very cool."

"We could do bold flavors, too," Alexis pointed out.

"That's just what I was thinking," I said. "You know I've been wanting to try that spicy chocolate recipe."

Alexis looked thoughtful. "This might be a

good time to try it, since we're giving away the cupcakes for free, anyway. We could do a test batch on Friday."

"Friday?" I asked. I had been so busy with Fashion Club that I wasn't as up on cupcake business as I should be.

"We've got to bake those cupcakes for Harriet's Hollow bookstore, remember?" Alexis asked. "She booked us a couple of months ago, and she wants fairy-themed cupcakes to go with a fairy-themed book display."

"Remember, we figured out the designs?" Katie asked. "One is a strawberry cupcake with pink frosting and a yellow-and-white fondant magic wand surrounded by glitter sprinkles. The other one is a vanilla cupcake with white icing and purple-and-pink fondant butterflies."

"Oh, right!" I said. It was all coming back to me. "So, I'll bring the chocolate and chili powder for the cupcakes."

"We need fondant, too," Alexis said. "Probably a whole pack of the mixed colors."

"I'm pretty sure I have that," I said.

"Okay, then we're set for Friday," Alexis said.

"We can do it at my house again," Katie offered.

"Sounds good," Alexis said. "Dylan had a fight

with Meredith and Skylar, and now she is in a bad mood, plus, she's home *all the time*. I need a break."

I nodded sympathetically. Alexis's older sister was basically nice, but I knew she could drive Alexis crazy.

I typed "CC cupcake baking Katie's house" into the calendar on my phone, so I wouldn't forget. I was feeling pretty organized—almost as organized as Alexis. Although really, I wasn't.

I sort of have an excuse. The next few days turned out to be totally crazy. I had soccer practice two days this week, and after school today, Beth and I walked around downtown and put up the fashion show posters. Thursday night after practice, Mom took me to get the ingredients for the spicy chocolate cupcakes. And when I wasn't doing all that stuff, I was doing tons of homework and trying to keep up the perfect child thing by cleaning up stuff without being asked.

On Friday, when we got to Katie's, we started out with the test batch of spicy chocolate cupcakes. We melted dark chocolate bits in the microwave and added some ancho chili powder, which is spicy but also has a nice, deep flavor. For the icing we went with a lighter chocolate frosting, spiced with a little red chili powder.

We baked the cupcakes, made the icing, and while we waited for the cupcakes to cool, we ate some Chinese food that Mrs. Brown had ordered for us.

"Mmm, spicy chicken and broccoli," Katie said, picking up her food with chopsticks.

Alexis shook her head. "You guys and your spicy food. Don't get me wrong; I think the spicy cupcakes are a good idea for a bold theme. But maybe we need to do a vanilla cupcake with just bold colors for the icing, for the wimps in the crowd like me."

"That's a good idea," I agreed. "Maybe we can do, like, a swirl of purple and turquoise or something. I'll try to sketch it out later."

Everyone nodded, and we went back to eating our Chinese food. After we cleaned up, we iced the spicy cupcakes. Then we cut one into pieces, so we could do a taste test.

"No, thank you," Alexis said, holding up her hand. "I trust your opinion."

I bit into mine. The icing was creamy, and the spiciness wasn't too hot—just enough to make my lips tingle. When we experiment with cupcakes on the first try, we don't always get it right, but I thought we had nailed it.

"I like it!" I announced.

Katie nodded. "Ith good," she agreed with her mouth full of cupcake.

"Spicy but not too spicy, and nice and choco-latey," Emma commented. "You really should try it, Alexis."

Alexis shook her head. "Thanks, but no thanks. We should get the fairy cupcakes started before it gets too late. I'll do both frostings."

"I can do the vanilla cupcake batter first," Katie volunteered. "Emma, can you chop up the straw-berries for the strawberry cupcakes?"

Emma nodded. "No problem."

"So, Mia, you should probably start rolling out and cutting the fondant," Alexis said. "These deco-rations are kind of complicated."

My stomach fell. "Um, I think I forgot to get the fondant," I said meekly. "I thought I had some at home, but I was wrong, and then I forgot to buy it when I went shopping."

Alexis raised an eyebrow. "Are you serious?"

"Maybe Mom can take us out to buy more," Katie quickly suggested, but I knew it was no use.

"We can't," I said, looking at the clock. "They only sell it at the bakery supply store, and that's closed now. I am so sorry, guys!"

Alexis shook her head. "Unbelievable."

"We must have some fondant in the pantry," Katie said, rushing to the closet in the kitchen where she and her mom kept all their baking supplies. She rummaged around for a minute and came out with a box of white fondant. "How about this?"

I looked inside the opened container. "We used about half already. But I could still make the wands, probably, and just paint them with yellow food coloring."

"What about the butterflies? They were going to be so pretty," Emma said a little sadly, and I felt even more terrible.

"Let me look and see what Katie has," I said, my brain spinning with ideas. "Is Harriet expecting butterflies?"

"Thankfully, no," Alexis replied. "She said she trusted us to make some nice fairy cupcakes."

"We're out of a lot of stuff, so we can't even make our own fondant," Katie told me as I headed into the closet. "I've been baking a lot lately."

I looked through the shelves, hoping to find some inspiration. Katie had colored sprinkles and glittery sprinkles, but the glittery ones were going on the magic wand cupcakes. She had mini chocolate candies, but those were not very fairylike, and some bins of gumdrops and other candy. And she had some red, green, and white cupcake papers left over from Christmas.

I grabbed the gumdrops. I picked out a pale yellow one and started slicing into it to make little sort of round pieces. They could look like butterfly wings, maybe, but I didn't love them.

Fairies . . . fairies . . . , I thought. I closed my eyes, thinking about all the fairy books I had read when I was little. *Fairies have wings and magic glitter, and they hang out on flowers and use toadstools for tables . . . That was it!*

"I have an idea," I said. "Katie, let's use these white cupcake papers for the vanilla cupcakes, okay?"

"Okay," Katie said, nodding.

"What are you going to do?" Alexis asked.

"I'm thinking we could make the cupcakes look like toadstools," I said. "They'll be perfect, because Harriet even has little chairs in her store that are painted like toadstools. Then we can do a layer of red frosting on top, and then dot them with white icing circles."

"That is kind of perfect," Emma said.

"I like it," agreed Katie.

"Let's do it, then," Alexis said. "I'll make a batch

of vanilla icing and dye most of it red, but leave some plain on the side for the dots."

I still felt bad about forgetting the fondant, but I felt a lot better once I had solved the problem. I got to work rolling out the white fondant for the magic wands, since it was going to take a lot of time to cut them out and paint them.

At one point I looked up from the fondant and saw Alexis whispering to Katie and Emma. Katie was giving me an *I'm so sorry* look.

I guess I was feeling a little frazzled, because then I sort of snapped.

"I'm sorry about the fondant, okay?" I said, looking right at Alexis. "How many times do you want me to apologize?"

Alexis looked up guiltily. "I didn't mean to talk behind your back," she said. "It's just, we can all see that this Fashion Club thing isn't really working out for you. It's interfering with the Cupcake Club."

"That is so not fair," I protested. "You're in the business club, and Emma has modeling and dog-walking jobs and is in band and everything."

"She only forgot the fondant this one time," Katie said, sticking up for me.

"I know, it's just . . ." Alexis's voice trailed off.

"The Fashion Club is new, and Beth isn't the most organized person in the world, and from the outside it seems like the club is kind of a mess."

"Well, the Cupcake Club would probably be a mess too, if we didn't have you," I pointed out. "Nobody is as organized as you. You're like a superhero with amazing organizing powers."

Katie and Emma started to giggle, and then I started giggling too. Alexis had a smirk on her face, and I could tell she thought it was funny too.

"I know that," Alexis replied. "It's who I am, and I'll own it. But you need to admit that the Fashion Club is a hot mess right now."

"Fine," I said. "It's true. But it's getting better. We have a place for the fashion show, and the posters are up, and the clothes are picked out."

"I believe you," Alexis said. "Just, if you need any help, let me know, okay?"

"Okay," I said, and I knew Alexis could probably be very helpful if we asked her. But there was a part of me that wanted to prove that we could do it on our own, you know?

"The vanilla cupcakes are ready for the oven," Katie announced, changing the subject. She's good at that.

Then Emma plugged her iPod into the little red

speaker on the kitchen counter, and the music got us pumped up as we worked. In the end the cupcakes looked fabulous. The magic wand cupcakes were pink and sparkly, and the toadstool cupcakes looked like they came out of a fairy tale.

"We are awesome," Alexis said, looking over the finished cupcakes in their carriers.

"Yes, we are," I said, and I felt good, because the cupcakes were perfect even though I had messed up—and things were cool between me and Alexis again. Smooth sailing. At least for now.

CHAPTER 13

My Secret Plan Is Busted

Saturday morning I had soccer, so Katie and Emma delivered the cupcakes to Harriet's Hollow. I was kind of jealous that I didn't get to go, but Katie sent me tons of photos. The cupcakes looked adorable with all of the books and fairy decorations that Harriet had set up, and Harriet loved them and made a big deal over them, which was nice.

After I got my soccer gear together, I climbed into the backseat of Mom's car. Mom and Eddie were in the front seat, arguing again.

"You've already had pizza two days this week," Mom was telling Eddie. "That's just not healthy."

"But I like pizza," Eddie said.

Mom turned around to look at me. "We're going to the Salad Factory for lunch, Mia," she informed me, and Eddie glanced at my mom and frowned a little.

Uh-oh, I thought. Maybe the perfect child thing I was doing wasn't enough. Had there been any unusual stress in the house lately? I wondered. Not really, except for my crazy schedule. Maybe that's what was stressing them out. But I couldn't help my schedule, could I? I mean, I like all the things I do outside school.

I'd just have to try harder to be more helpful, I resolved. When we got to the Salad Factory, Mom and Eddie were smiling and stuff again, but to be honest, it didn't really sink in that they were getting along. I was too worried about the possibility that they might get divorced or something. That's all I could think of as I ate my salad of lettuce, avocado, broccoli, chicken, and shredded cheese.

When we got home I took a quick shower, and then I made sure to put my dirty soccer uniform in the laundry room. When I was dressed, I got out the vacuum cleaner and started to vacuum the living room rug. Tiki and Milkshake usually get their little white hairs all over it, so it needs to be vacuumed a lot. I usually complain when Mom asks me to do it, but that was before.

When I finished and put the vacuum cleaner back in the closet, Mom called out to me.

"Mia, can you please come see us in the kitchen?"

I went into the kitchen and saw her and Eddie sitting at the kitchen table. Of course, I started to worry.

This is it, I thought. *They're going to tell me they're splitting up.*

I was shaking a little bit as I sat down at the table.

"What is it?" I asked.

"Mia, we're wondering what you're up to," Mom said frankly, and I was surprised. "You've been so . . . *helpful* lately. Not that that's a bad thing—it's good. But it's a little suspicious. At first we thought you did it because you wanted the Women's Club's space for your fashion show, but then you kept on doing it."

"Shouldn't I be insulted?" I asked. "You're acting like I've never done anything nice before."

"Of course you have," Eddie said. "But you're like a cleaning machine these days. What's up?"

I looked at Mom and Eddie. Could I really tell them what I'd been thinking?

"Come on," Eddie pressed. "Is it another pair of expensive shoes?"

100

That really did insult me, and I angrily blurted out, "No!" I turned to Mom. "It's because you and Eddie had that big fight about Eddie's sister or whatever, and it reminded me of you and Dad when you were fighting before you got divorced, and then I thought maybe you and Eddie were going to break up, and . . ."

I almost started to cry, but I kept it in. I just stopped talking, because I was afraid to say more out loud. Then I sighed.

"I know people get divorced because there's stress, so I thought if there was no stress . . ."

Mom and Eddie looked at each other, surprised. I saw Mom take a really deep breath.

"I'm so sorry we argued in front of you," Mom said in a gentle voice. "We're adults, and we shouldn't do that. But please don't be worried. In any relationship people will argue. We get cranky and stressed out sometimes. It happens to everyone, but Eddie and I always talk things out. We have a strong relationship, and you don't have to worry."

They both looked at me. I believed them, but there was a little part of me that was still a little worried.

Then Eddie gave Mom a squeeze. "I love this lady, Mia. She's not getting away from me. You've got nothing to worry about." He planted a big kiss on her, and she started to giggle.

I went from sad to grossed out in two seconds flat. I hate it when Eddie and Mom get all gooey and in love like that. (Even if it means they're not breaking up.)

"Okay, okay, I get it!" I yelled, making a face.

Mom and Eddie laughed.

"I hope the next time you're worried about something you'll tell us about it, or at least one of us," Mom said. "Is everything else okay?"

I thought about my answer. "Well, Dad and his girlfriend, Lynne, broke up. And I guess that made me a little sad."

Mom gave Eddie a knowing look. "I understand. Maybe that brought back some bad memories for you, *mija*."

Mom gave me a big, long hug, and I felt a lot better.

"Of course, if you want to keep cleaning, we won't stop you," Eddie joked.

I broke away from Mom, laughing. "Maybe," I said. "But if I go back to my old habits, don't be surprised!"

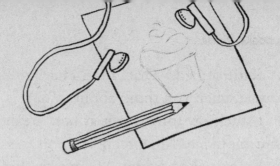

CHAPTER 14

Olivia Strikes Again

Once I knew that Mom and Eddie weren't going to get divorced or anything, I felt really happy. I spent the rest of the weekend sketching and listening to music, and when Katie came onto the bus Monday morning, I had in my earbuds and was bopping my head to the song.

Katie started moving her lips, but I couldn't hear her, so I took out my earbuds.

"What did you say?" I asked.

"I said, 'You're in a good mood today,'" Katie repeated. "And it's Monday. You hate Mondays."

"Hey, that's right," I said, and then I lowered my voice. "I talked to Mom and Eddie about . . . you know, what I was worried about. But everything's okay."

Katie smiled. "That's nice. They are a pretty cute couple when you think about it."

I stuck my tongue out at her. "Yeah, and so are your mom and Mr. Green."

Katie looked around. "Don't say that so loud!"

"Sorry," I said. "But everybody knows, anyway, right?"

"Yes, but I'm hoping they'll forget it," Katie replied.

Then Katie and I started talking about other stuff besides parents, and I was still in a good mood for the rest of the day—even when Beth came up to me in the hall.

"We're moving the Fashion Club meeting to Wednesday this week because Olivia can't make it," she told me.

"Um, okay," I replied, thinking quickly. I still felt a little bad about flaking out about the fondant, so I didn't want to miss another Cupcake Club meeting. "I can't go. But text me if there's anything you need me to do."

"Sure," Beth said, and as she walked away I got a tiny bit worried. Not that I'm an awesome organizer or anything, but I liked to think I helped out at the meetings by keeping us on track. But I pushed that worry aside. All the important decisions had been made already, so it wouldn't hurt if I missed the meeting.

On Wednesday we had our Cupcake Club meeting after school at Alexis's house. Since we weren't baking anything, we went up to her room, which, as you can probably imagine, is just as organized as she is.

"Okay, so I was hoping we could discuss some new advertising strategies," Alexis began. "We could use a few more jobs in the next few months, and we need to drum up business."

"Should we do new flyers?" Emma asked. "We could put them in mailboxes again."

"I was thinking that," Alexis said, "but the printing costs can add up. So I looked up the ad rates in the *Maple Grove Gazette*. We can put in an ad for sixty dollars and reach even more people than we could with the flyers."

"That's a good idea," Katie said.

I nodded. "We'd have to design something that really stands out, so people don't just turn the page and miss it."

"Or we could come up with a slogan stands out," Katie said. "Like, 'Hey, you! You need a cupcake!'"

We all laughed, and suddenly Alexis's older sister, Dylan, was in the room. She put her hands on the sides of her head.

"Could you all *please* be quiet," she said dramatically. "I have a huge headache."

"You *are* a huge headache," Alexis said under her breath.

"I heard that," Dylan snapped, and then she went back to her room.

"See what I mean?" Alexis said. "She'd better make up with Meredith and Skylar soon. This is driving me crazy."

We talked about the ad some more. I made some sketches of what the ad could look like, and then Eddie came and picked up Katie and me.

That night I didn't get a text from Beth about the Fashion Club meeting, and I thought about texting her, except I felt really, really tired for some reason. I went to bed, like, two hours earlier than usual, and when I woke up I had a cold! A totally gross, nose-blowing, sneezing, sore throat cold.

"Well, you are not going to school today," Mom said as soon as she saw me. "I was planning to work from home today, anyway."

The whole day Thursday I was miserable. I slept a lot, and Mom made me chicken soup, and finally in the afternoon I felt good enough to go downstairs and watch TV. The next morning I felt tons better, but Mom still wanted me to stay home.

"But I've got to go see Dad today," I protested.

Mom frowned. "I don't know, Mia. You're still coughing, and I don't want you traveling if you're sick. You don't want to get your father sick, either."

I started to tear up a little, probably because I didn't feel good. "But I haven't seen him in two weeks."

Mom sighed. "I'll discuss it with him. Let's see how you are later."

I showered and got dressed and tried to feel better—and I did, mostly. Katie stopped by after school with my homework (but Mom wouldn't let me go near her) and then at four o'clock I heard the bell ring while I was on the couch watching TV.

I heard Mom answer the door, and then Dad walked into the living room.

"Dad!" I cried, running up to give him a hug.

He smiled. "You look better than I thought you would, *mija*."

"Thanks," I said. "But what are you doing here?"

"I drove in to pick you up for the weekend," he replied. Dad has a car that he keeps in a garage and uses for business trips and sometimes to come see me play soccer. But the train is faster and easier, so mostly I take the train. "Your mom doesn't want you on the train. She will let you come as long as you promise to stay in the apartment and do your homework."

"I promise!" I said. "Let me go get ready."

Maybe I was antsy from being in the house for two days, but I really wanted to go with Dad. I quickly packed my bags, kissed Mom good-bye (on the cheek, so she wouldn't get sick), and Dad and I headed out.

Since we couldn't go out for sushi, Dad ordered for delivery some sushi, along with a nice big container of miso soup. Saturday I felt better, but I stayed in and did homework, and then Dad and I did a *Lord of the Rings* movie marathon, which was really fun. I love the costumes in those movies, and I sketched the whole time. We ordered in turkey sandwiches and matzo ball soup for lunch, and for dinner we had Indian food delivered (which I like because it's spicy). That's one of the great things about Manhattan—you can practically get anything in the world delivered right to your door.

By the time Dad drove me home on Sunday I felt loads better. As I unpacked in my bedroom, I suddenly remembered that I still hadn't heard from Beth. I shot her a quick text.

How did the meeting go? Need me 2 do anything?

I expected Beth to text back, but instead she gave me a call.

"Hey, Mia," she said. "I heard you were sick."

"Just a cold," I replied.

"Oh, good," Beth said. "So, I was going to text you, but it's kind of a whole long thing. We decided to do a new theme for the show."

I thought I must be hearing wrong. "You what?"

"Yeah," Beth replied. "'Fun and Flirty.'"

Of course—that was the theme Olivia had suggested before we decided on "Bold Moves." "But I thought we decided the clothes we picked didn't go with the theme."

"Well, yeah," Beth said. "So we went back to the mall and picked out all new clothes. Olivia found a new dress for you. It's pretty nice. I'll text you the picture."

My head was spinning. "Are you serious?" I asked, my voice getting loud. "The fashion show is less than a week away. This is kind of a bad time to change everything around, isn't it? And I told the

Cupcake Club about the bold theme, and we made test cupcakes already and everything."

"Yeah, well, like, Chelsea and Jasmine thought it was a bad idea to change, but Olivia kind of over-ruled everyone, you know?" Beth asked.

I sighed. "Yes, I know."

"And, anyway, hopefully the cupcakes aren't a big deal, right? I mean, they're just cupcakes," Beth said.

It was no use explaining to Beth about my spicy cupcakes or how it takes time and money to do a test batch. I just wanted to get off the phone.

"Yeah, well, bye then," I said, and I hung up.

I was fuming by now. I stormed downstairs into the kitchen, where Mom was cutting up carrots for dinner.

"You are not going to believe this!" I said, and then I told Mom what had happened. "This is ridiculous. I am so quitting this stupid fashion show. I can't take it anymore."

"Take a deep breath now, Mia," Mom said. She nodded to the chair next to her. "Come on. Sit down."

I did what she said, mostly because ranting about everything had calmed me down a little bit.

"I just want to quit," I repeated, calmer this time.

"It's not fair. Olivia did everything behind my back because she knew nobody else would stand up to her. She probably just didn't want me to wear that dress—the only good dress in the place."

"What dress does she have you wearing now?" Mom asked.

I looked at my phone. "Let me check."

Beth had texted the picture of the dress. It was this pale pink flowery print with cap sleeves and ruffles around the waist.

"Gross," I said, handing Mom the phone.

Mom nodded. "Pale pink is not your best color," she agreed. "And I don't love the ruffles, but they're trending now. It's a cute shape, though, and with styling we could make it look great on you. Why don't you tell Beth that you'll pick out a new dress yourself? I can go with you and find something that's still great."

"You should have seen the green dress," I said. "I looked gorgeous in it."

Mom nodded again. "Normally, I'd advise you to talk to Olivia and try to restore things to the way they were," she said, "but there simply isn't time. I understand if you don't want to be in the show, but it will be difficult for me to explain to the Women's Club why my daughter isn't in it."

I hadn't thought of that. "I don't know," I said. "I am so mad at Olivia right now, I don't even want to look at her, much less be in a club with her."

"I get it," Mom said. "But, you know, that's just how it is in business too. I have had to work with quite a few people who made my job way more difficult than it had to be or who wanted to control everything themselves. Learning how to deal with those kind of people is good experience."

"You sound like Alexis," I said.

"So, what do you think?" Mom asked.

I sighed. "I'll do it. But I *hate* this theme."

"Tell you what," Mom said. "Tomorrow after school let's go look at the dresses in person. Then we'll work out some styling ideas together, okay? I'm sure we can make it work."

I felt a little better. "I hope so," I said.

CHAPTER 15

Style Solves Everything

$\mathcal{T}$he next day was a typical Monday. When Katie found me on the bus that morning, I was drawing a thunderstorm in my sketchbook instead of bopping around to music. She knew what was up as soon as she looked at me.

"Miserable Monday, huh?" she asked.

"I don't feel like talking about it," I said truthfully. I knew I had to break the news to the Cupcake Club that the theme had changed, but I didn't want to tell the whole thing twice. Luckily, Katie understands that kind of thing. She leaned around the seat and talked to George Martinez the whole time, and I kept on sketching black clouds and lightning bolts.

Maybe I haven't mentioned it yet, but I have

Olivia in a bunch of my classes. She kept looking at me, like she was waiting for me to say something about the new theme, but I didn't give her the satisfaction. I totally managed to ignore her until lunchtime.

Beth came up to our table as soon as we started eating, and Olivia was staring at us, curious to see what was going on.

"So, Mia, I hope everything's cool with the new theme," she said.

"It's fine," I said as coolly as I could. "Listen, my mom offered to help us out. She and I are going to Trendz to check out the clothes in person, and she's going to give us some styling ideas. And she'll help me pick out a dress that fits the theme." I was okay with going with the theme, but there was no way I was letting Olivia pick out my dress.

"Awesome," Beth said. "She's a professional stylist, right?"

Suddenly Olivia appeared behind her. "Wait a second, shouldn't we vote on that? We should be styling the clothes ourselves."

"No way! This is great," Beth said. "We haven't even had time to talk about styling, anyway. Thanks, Mia."

Beth walked away, completely oblivious to how furious Olivia was. Olivia glared at me and then followed her.

And then my friends went crazy.

"She changed the theme?" Alexis asked. "A week before the show?"

"Oh no! And we made those delicious test cupcakes," Emma remarked.

"I know, I know," I said. "It's all Olivia's fault, and I missed the meeting, and then I got sick and couldn't stop her."

"This doesn't give us much time to come up with new cupcakes," Alexis said, anxiously tapping her fork against her food tray. "What's the new theme?"

"'Fun and Flirty,' but it doesn't matter," I replied. "It's not fair for us to have to redo things on short notice. We just won't do the cupcakes. We were doing them a favor, anyway."

Alexis raised an eyebrow. "'Them'? Does that mean you're not in the club anymore?"

"I'm doing the fashion show, but I don't know if I'll stay after that," I admitted. "You guys were right. It's a terrible club."

"We never said it was terrible," Emma protested. "And, anyway, you guys are just getting

115

started. We messed things up all the time when we first began our business."

"We still do," Katie said, and we all laughed.

"Anyway, just forget about it, please?" I asked. "Olivia's right. Cupcakes and fashion don't mix."

Alexis shot one of her looks at Katie and Emma, but I ignored it. I mean, everybody was at least nice about it. Alexis had every right to start insulting the Fashion Club, but she didn't do that, and I appreciated that.

Mom kept her promise and we went to the mall that night after dinner. She got a funny look on her face as we entered the store, with its colored lights pulsing and music blasting outside.

"Interesting choice," she said.

"Olivia's choice," I reminded her.

Luckily we found Nikki working by the register again.

"Oh hi," she said, recognizing me right away. "You're one of those fashion girls, right?"

"Um, yeah," I said. "This is my mom. We were hoping to take a look at the new clothes the other girls picked out."

"That was kind of crazy, right?" Nikki said. "They came in over the weekend with that one bossy girl and picked out all new stuff."

She led us to a rack of clothes by the dressing room with a sign that read ON HOLD taped to it. I couldn't help noticing that Nikki was looking pretty stylish again. She had on a dress with a print of little green flowers, topped with a cropped black sweater. Then I noticed the ruffles around the waist and realized something.

"Hey, that looks like the pink dress Olivia picked out for me," I said. I moved to the rack and quickly found the pale pink flowered dress. "So it comes in other colors?"

Nikki nodded. "This green, and, like, an electric blue. I can show you."

"The green would be nicer with your coloring," Mom suggested.

"That's what I was thinking," I said, and I followed Nikki back over to a rack of dresses. She pulled out a green one in my size.

"Would it be okay if I switched the pink dress with this one?" I asked.

Nikki shrugged. "Sure."

I took the dress back to the rack, where Mom was busy looking through the clothes and making notes in a little notepad.

"I'll take pictures of everything," I told her.

"Mia, I think this could be a really cute

collection," she said. "It just needs a little finessing, that's all."

"So, um, when were you guys going to pick these up and bring them back?" Nikki asked. "I asked that other girl, and she said she would call me, but she didn't."

I looked at Mom helplessly. Things were such a total mess!

"We'll come by on Saturday morning when you open and get them back to you on Sunday," she said.

Nikki nodded. "Cool."

Then I thought of something. "You should come to the show. It's free," I told Nikki. "You've been really nice about everything."

"Aw, that's so cute of you guys," Nikki said. "Where is it supposed to be?"

I gave her the info, and Mom and I finished up taking pictures and stuff.

"We should probably go," Mom said. "It's a school night, after all." She said it right in front of Nikki, which was totally embarrassing, but Nikki didn't laugh or anything.

"Cool. See you Saturday," she said.

As Mom and I drove home, I realized how lucky I was to have her as a mom.

"Thanks, Mom," I said. "Any time something goes wrong, you always make it better."

"You're that way too, Mia," she said, smiling at me. "You're a very caring girl."

"I am?"

Mom nodded. "Of course. Like when you thought Eddie and I were having trouble and you tried to fix it. You're that way with your friends, too. But, you know, sometimes it's okay to ask for help. You don't have to fix everything by yourself."

I had never really thought about it much, but Mom was right. Like, when things were tough between Katie and her ex–best friend, Callie, I helped to smooth things out. And even when I forgot the fondant, I made sure to fix it so that we still had fairy cupcakes.

"Thanks," I said. "Between us, we will probably need both of our superhelpful powers to make this fashion show work."

I was kidding, but I ended up being right—mostly. As it turned out it would take a whole team of people with superhelping powers to save the fashion show!

CHAPTER 16

"Wing It"? Are You Serious?

Olivia made sure the next Fashion Club meeting was on a Wednesday, but I made sure to go to it, even if it meant missing a Cupcake meeting. It was the last meeting before the fashion show, and I wanted to confirm that Olivia didn't make any more crazy changes.

As usual, Olivia started talking at the start of the meeting, just like she was the president, but Beth didn't seem to mind.

"So, we all know about our new theme," Olivia said. "Chelsea, you picked out new music, right?"

Chelsea frowned. "I don't know how to pick out 'fun and flirty' music."

"That's okay, I've got a lot of good songs on my iPod," Olivia said, and Chelsea frowned again.

I guessed I wasn't the only one who was unhappy about the theme change.

"So, Mia's mom is going to help us style the clothes," Beth announced. "She, like, styles famous people."

"Sometimes," I said, trying to play it down, but actually I'm really proud of what my mom does. I just don't like to brag about it. "We went to Trendz the other night and took some pictures. Mom put together some ideas, if you want to see."

"Sure," Beth said, and I took out a notebook Mom had prepared for me. She'd pasted a photo of each dress or outfit on a page, and then she'd either sketched her accessory ideas or added photos of some things she had that she was going to lend us.

"Like, here's the dress I'm wearing," I said, pointing to the page. "Mom's idea was to pair it with this blue cropped sweater I have, and silver bangles, and she had the idea to wear heels with little blue ankle socks."

"Looks pretty flirty to me," Julia remarked.

"But I picked out a pink flowered dress for you," Olivia blurted out.

"The green looks better on me," I said simply.

Libby nodded. "Definitely."

Everyone got excited looking through the book.

Julia had a great necklace that would go with Beth's outfit, and Jasmine had a scarf that she knew would go perfectly with the dress she was going to wear.

"Mom says she'll come backstage and help us put our outfits together," I informed everyone.

"I still say we should be doing this on our own," Olivia said.

"It's nice of Mia's mom to help us," Julia countered.

"And let's face it, we could use some help getting this thing off the ground," said Libby.

"Fine," Olivia said. "Anyway, we need to talk about other stuff. Like how much we're going to charge at the door."

"We're charging at the door?" I asked.

Olivia nodded. "We decided it at the last meeting, when you couldn't make it. We can use the money when we go to New York City."

"That's a good idea," I said. "Except the posters don't say anything about admission. People are expecting a free show."

Olivia picked up one of the posters, examined it, and scowled. "Well, so what?" she asked. "I'm sure they won't mind supporting a school group."

"But you have to tell them in advance," I said, and I could hear my voice getting louder. Olivia is one of the only people who can make me lose my cool, and I hate that! I tried to calm down.

Luckily, Libby had an idea. "Well, we could ask for a donation. Like they do at a museum."

"That's actually not a bad idea," I agreed. "If people don't want to pay, they don't have to, but I bet a lot of them will. We just need somebody to collect donations at the door."

"One of us can do it," Olivia suggested.

"We can't, because we'll all be backstage getting ready to model," I shot back.

"I'm not modeling," Chelsea said. "I can do it."

"See?" Olivia said, shooting me a look.

"I thought Chelsea was going to play the music when the fashion show starts," I said.

"She can do both," Olivia said. "It's no big deal."

The meeting was starting to sound like a tennis match between me and Olivia. Every time she suggested something, I thought of a problem with it, and she had an answer for it.

I think we were making Beth anxious, because she said, "Well, it looks like we're all set for Saturday."

I couldn't believe it. "Are you sure?" I asked. "I mean, I've never run a fashion show, but I've done events with the Cupcake Club before, and there's usually a bunch of stuff we have to figure out. Like when we're getting there to set up and how we'll handle cleanup and where things are going to go. Don't we need to figure out where the models are going to line up and stuff like that?"

"Oh, right." Beth sat back down. "We were going to go visit the club to check it out, and I totally forgot. Do you think we can get there early and figure it out then?"

I nodded. "Probably. I'll ask my mom."

"So, then, let's try to get there at, like, four, and we'll figure it out when we get there," Beth said. "We can wing it."

"Wing it"? Had she actually said that? If we ever "winged it" at a Cupcake event, we'd have no clients. I started to panic.

"We should at least get a list together of what everybody is doing and bringing," I suggested, trying desperately to think of what Alexis would do in this situation.

"Why don't you get that together and e-mail all of us?" Olivia asked.

That wasn't what I had in mind, but I guess it was better than nothing. "Well, yeah, um, I guess I can do that."

"Cool. See everybody on Saturday," Beth said, standing up again.

I left the meeting feeling kind of worried, so the first thing I did when I got home was type up the list.

Setup, 4:00, Saturday: All FC members
Decorations: Was Julia bringing balloons and Beth bringing flowers? I forget.
Models: Beth, Olivia, Libby, Jasmine, Mia, Julia, Callie, Maggie, Bella, Mikayla, Lucy, Sophie
Models get dressed: 6:00
Doors open: 6:30
Donations at front door: Chelsea
Music: Prepared by Olivia, run by Chelsea
Emcee: We didn't think of this. Beth since she's president?
Cleanup: All FC members

It wasn't the way Alexis would do a list, but it looked pretty good to me. I e-mailed it to the FC members right away. Beth e-mailed me back "Cool!" and Julia sent a smiley face. Nobody else responded, and that wasn't a good sign.

I sighed. I had done everything I could. Now there was nothing to do but "wing it" and hope for the best!

CHAPTER 17

Cupcake Club to the Rescue!

$\mathcal{M}$om and I got to the Women's Club's room at four o'clock on Saturday. Mom had a key so she could open up the place. We walked into the big open space that the craft fair had been held in. Dozens of folding chairs were stacked up against one wall.

"The other girls should be here soon," I said a little nervously.

"Well, we can start bringing in the clothes," Mom said. "There's a room to the side that will make a good setup area for the models. Everyone can change in the back bathroom."

We had gone to the mall in the morning and picked up all the clothes. Now we unloaded them from the back of Mom's car. Each time I carried in a load of the heavy clothing, I looked at the clock. Where was everybody?

Finally, at four thirty, Julia walked in carrying a bouquet of wrapped-up pink carnations.

"Hey, Mia," she said, and then I introduced her to my mom. Then Julia held up the flowers. "So, what should we do with these?"

"Um, I'm not sure," I said. "I actually thought you were supposed to bring balloons."

"I thought your e-mail said flowers," Julia replied with a shrug. She looked around. "I guess I need a vase or something."

"Why don't you girls concentrate on setting up the chairs?" Mom suggested. "Once everything is arranged, I'll bet you'll know exactly where to put the flowers."

"How should we set them up?" I asked.

Mom looked around the room. "Well, you won't have a proper runway for the show. But I'd still do a wide aisle in the middle of the room. And leave some space by the back, where the models will step out, so everyone will have a good view of the models when they first come out."

"That makes sense," Julia and I agreed, and we started setting up the folding chairs in rows on either side of the room. As I set up chair after chair

I looked at the clock again. It was getting late.

"Is Chelsea coming soon?" I asked Julia, because I knew she and Chelsea were friends.

"Oh, she has a cold," Julia said. "She can't come, but she says good luck."

I stopped. "What? But she's supposed to be at the front door. And work the music."

"Well, maybe I could do it," Julia suggested.

"But you're modeling," I said. "We're all modeling!"

I was starting to panic, and that's when Olivia breezed in.

"Oh, so you were just going to set it up yourselves?" she asked.

I couldn't believe her. "We were supposed to all get here at four. It's after five. We needed to get started."

"Whatever," Olivia said. She took her iPod out of her purse. "So, where can I plug this in?"

"I don't know," I replied. "I thought you and Chelsea had that worked out. And Chelsea's not coming. She has a cold."

"Calm down," Olivia said. "I'll just text Callie and tell her to bring her speakers when she comes." Olivia typed into her phone. "So, where are the clothes?"

I nodded to the door in the back of the room. "Through there."

Then things started to get crazy. Beth got there next, followed by Libby and Jasmine.

"Sorry we're late," Libby said, "but my mom drove both of us, and I had a swim meet and it went late."

Beth looked around the room. "Wow, it looks good in here. Thanks." Then she held out a bunch of flowers wrapped in paper. "So, is there a vase for these or something?"

"You brought flowers too," I stated. Of course. "Um, I don't think there's a vase. But maybe we can do something cool with all the flowers."

"Maybe we could tie some flowers to the chair at the end of each row," Julia said. "I saw that at my aunt's wedding."

"That would actually look pretty," I said. "Only we need ribbon. Let me go ask my mom."

I found Mom in the back room. "Olivia's getting changed," she said. "How's the setup going?"

I explained about the flower idea, and Mom found some ribbon for us in one of the closets. Beth, Julia, Libby, Jasmine, and I worked together to attach the flowers, and they did look really pretty.

Just as we finished, Lucy and Sophie came into

the room. They're friends with the Cupcake Club, but since they're, like, mega best friends, they mostly hang out together. They were followed by a girl with curly dark hair who looked a lot like Julia.

"Mikayla!" Julia ran and gave her a hug, and I realized this must be the cousin she was talking about.

Before I could send the models to the back room, Olivia came out in her outfit. She had on one of those supershort skirts from Trendz—a pink one—and a white sleeveless top with lace around the collar. My mom had added a short boyfriend blazer that had a small pink-flowered print, and Olivia's dangly earrings had a pearl on each end. She looked totally adorable.

"How do I look?" she asked, and everybody swarmed around her, complimenting her.

"You look sooooo cute!" Julia exclaimed.

"Fun and flirty," Libby remarked.

"I can't wait to see what we're going to wear," Lucy said. "Can we get changed too?"

She asked nobody in particular, but I kind of felt like I was in charge at this point.

"Well, the space is set up. We just need a table in the front," I answered, and then I remembered we had no one to sit at the table. Or a speaker for the music. "Olivia, is Callie coming soon with the speaker?'

"Oh, Callie and Maggie aren't coming," Olivia said. "They had some, like, drama club practice or something."

You know how people say "that was the last straw"? Meaning they can't take it anymore? That's exactly how I felt.

I didn't freak out. I didn't even say anything. I just walked to the nearest folding chair and sat down.

Nobody noticed. They all followed Olivia into the back to change. I thought I might start crying when the door opened again.

"Mia, it looks so nice in here!"

It was Katie, holding a cupcake carrier! Alexis and Emma came in behind her, and they were holding carriers too.

"What did you—I mean, what are you guys doing here?" I asked.

"We couldn't let you do your fashion show without cupcakes," Katie replied. "You aren't mad, are you?"

I jumped up and hugged her. "No way! You guys are awesome!"

"We should set up in that corner," Alexis said, nodding to the right. "I'll go get a table."

Seeing my friends made me feel so much better.

"How's everything going?" Emma asked.

"Well, not so great, I guess," I admitted. "We're missing models, and we have no one to work the door and no way to play music. It's a disaster. You guys were right all along. I never should have done this."

"That's not true!" Katie said. "It looks nice in here. And you have clothes and stuff, right?"

I nodded. "Yeah, I guess."

Alexis put her cupcakes on the table she had set up and walked over.

"We can help you with all that stuff you mentioned," she said.

"Of course we can!" Emma added.

I hesitated. I had wanted so badly to prove I could handle the whole Fashion Club thing on my own. But then I remembered something Mom had said, about how I don't have to fix everything myself all the time.

"That would be great," I said.

Alexis immediately went into business mode. "For some reason Dylan said she was coming to this thing, so I'll text her and tell her to bring my iPod speakers. I can work the front door too. Are you selling tickets?"

I shook my head. "No, we didn't put it on the poster. We're accepting donations, though."

"Great, then you won't need change. Let me set something up," she said, and then hurried off.

"And I can model for you," Emma offered.

"Oh, that would be perfect!" I squealed. "But I still need one more."

Emma and I both looked at Katie. She held up her hands and started to back away.

"Ohhh, no," she said. "I do not model. Look at me!"

Katie had come dressed in her Cupcake Club T-shirt, ripped jeans, and a pair of sneakers that she had painted with rainbow designs.

"We have clothes for you," I told her. "All you have to do is put them on and walk. That's it."

"You have to do it," Emma said. "I'll help you."

"Pleeeeeease?" I begged.

Katie sighed. "All right! All right! But if I trip and fall on my face, then I told you so."

I looked at the clock and realized I should probably get changed too. I grabbed my out-fit and went into the bathroom to get changed. When I came out, Katie was standing in front of me wearing a frilly, yellow cheetah-print dress and making a face.

"I look ridiculous," she said.

She was kind of right, but I didn't want to let on that it was true. Katie is really cute, but that dress wouldn't look good on anybody.

"Let's see what my mom can do," I said, and we went into the back room. Mom was working it like the pro she is.

"Lucy, take off that necklace! It doesn't work. Julia and Mikayla, switch scarves!"

I tapped her on the shoulder. "Mom."

She turned and saw Katie, and her eyebrows went up. "Wow, that is some dress. Let's see what we can do."

Olivia came over. "Oh, that dress—"

"I know," said Mom. "It's pretty bad, but I'm a professional. I can fix it."

Olivia's face fell, and everything was kind of worth it for that one minute.

Since my outfit was all set, I went to the front to see what was happening. Alexis was expertly handling the crowd at the door. I was kind of surprised by how many people had showed up.

"Admission is free, but the Fashion Club appreciates your donations," Alexis was saying, and the woman in front of her opened her purse and dropped five bucks into the donation can Alexis had fashioned for us. I realized it was Mrs. Carr, the English teacher. I also saw Nikki on line, as well as Mrs. Barrows from the Women's Club, and a bunch of girls from school.

Feeling nervous, I rushed to the back room. "There are a lot of people out there," I said.

"We should start lining you all up," Mom said. "Did you work out the order?"

I shook my head, and Mom looked at her watch. "I'd better do it, if you don't mind."

"No, do it," I said, relieved. "Beth is going to introduce us, so maybe she should be the last to walk, so it all comes around full circle."

Mom nodded. "That'll work."

The next half hour was a blur as we all put finishing touches on our outfits and Mom lined us up. I was glad that she put me right between Katie and Emma. Emma looked adorable in a light blue flowered dress, and Mom had given Katie a cardigan to wear that really toned down the cheetah print. Emma had lent Katie the flats she was wearing, so that Katie wouldn't have to worry about walking down the runway.

Alexis came into the room. "You guys ready?

Cupcake Diaries

Dylan brought my speakers. Whose iPod are we using?"

Olivia ran up to her. "Here it is. It's the Fun and Flirty playlist."

"Got it," Alexis said, and then she ran out.

I turned to Beth. "Okay, this is it."

Beth nodded. She didn't look nervous at all. "Cool."

Beth walked into the main room, and we heard all the chatting die down. We couldn't see Beth, but we could hear her.

"Welcome to the first ever fashion show by the Fashion Club," she announced in her usual calm voice. "We worked really hard on this, and we hope to do more in the future. All the clothes are from Trendz in the mall, so if you like what you see, you can get them there. The theme of the show is 'Fun and Flirty.'"

Alexis started the music, and Beth returned to the back room. Olivia was first on line, so she headed out into the main space. This time we kept the door open so we could watch.

I have to say she nailed it. She walked to the start of the "runway" and did a few poses so everyone could get a good look. Then she walked back to the end of the runway and did a few more poses.

When she walked off, everybody clapped.

The music was pumping, and we all got into the spirit—even Katie. She didn't do any poses, but she managed to smile the whole way down.

"That was weird!" she hissed quietly when she passed me.

As I walked out, I knew what she meant. It looked like every chair was filled, and I felt like every single eye was looking at me. Honestly, I don't know how Emma does it.

After we had all walked the runway once, we went out as a group in one long line. People clapped and cheered, and that felt good. Then Beth announced, "Thanks, everyone! Please enjoy some cupcakes donated by the Cupcake Club!"

I couldn't believe how well everything had gone, despite all the problems we had. Nikki was really happy with the attention the store got, everyone loved the cupcakes, and Alexis booked us a birthday party, but the best thing was that Mrs. Carr talked to us afterward.

"I'm amazed that you girls did this on your own," she said.

"Actually, we needed a lot of help," Beth admitted, and I was glad to hear her say it. "Mia's mom came to our rescue, and we made a lot of mistakes besides."

"I would be happy to be your adviser if you think you need one," she offered.

"Yes!" I said quickly, and the other girls agreed—even Olivia, to my amazement.

Afterward, Mom made sure everyone in the club helped clean up—even Olivia—and Katie, Alexis, and Emma even stayed to help us, because that's how nice they are.

"That was a really fun show," Emma remarked when we were all done.

"Thanks," I said. "But I couldn't have done it without you guys."

"No problem," Katie said. "Just don't ever ask me to model again."

We all laughed, and I felt really happy about how things had worked out. Things were smooth again, but now I know that if they ever get a little bumpy, it's okay. There are people to help me smooth things over. And one thing I knew for sure: Despite what Olivia thought, cupcakes and fashion are a fabulous mix!

Want another sweet cupcake?
Here's a sneak peek
of the nineteenth book in the

CUPCAKE 🧁 DIARIES

series:

Emma:
lights! camera!
cupcakes!

The Topic of the Town

$\mathcal{I}$ love Fridays! Almost every Friday, my three best friends—Alexis, Mia, and Katie—and I have an official meeting and baking session for our Cupcake Club. Each week we try rotate where it takes place, so that makes it a little more interesting, and a lot of times we stretch it out into a sleepover too. It's just fun and kind of relaxing to know I don't have to worry about Friday plans. I'm always guaranteed to be chilling with my BFFs! It's also pretty cool to have something to look forward to all week.

Some weeks we have very little business to cover, but this week we had a lot! Alexis ran the meeting as usual.

"First on the agenda is a cupcake competition—birthday party for Isabel Gormley in two weeks.

She'd like two dozen unfrosted cupcakes; a mix of vanilla and chocolate—so half are chocolate cake and the other half are yellow cake. Then we'll send the frosting on the side, vanilla and chocolate. They are going to have a contest so all the kids can ice and decorate the cupcakes themselves."

"That is so cute!" cried Mia, lounging on my TV room sofa. "Wouldn't she maybe like some fondant roses on a sheet? Or containers of toppings?"

It's become almost boring for us to make basic cupcakes; we do it so rarely. We've made so many over-the-top cupcake designs in our day. Mia is very creative idea-wise, and Katie is great at execution. Alexis makes sure we charge properly for them. I'm good at promoting and networking to get us jobs.

"Actually, it would be cool to create a cupcake competition kit for parties. Maybe we could advertise that on our website!" I said.

Alexis tapped her pen with her teeth. "I agree. If we could get the pricing right, it might be worth offering it for a limited time to see how it does." She made some notes in her book. She's very strategic with how we spend our money, which is a good thing.

"Should we tint the vanilla frosting at least?"

suggested Katie. "We can give them different colors, like pink or purple . . . ?"

Alexis made some notes in her book. "I'll e-mail Mrs. Gormley and ask her, and also I'll see if she wants us to create the kit for them. The Gormleys are good clients. She'll probably be up for it."

I nodded. "What else is in the lineup?"

"We have the PTA meeting coming up, so let's do a complimentary order with fliers or little cards with our contact info to hand out. Maybe two dozen minis, since the parents don't eat much. Then"—Alexis consulted her notes—"we have a retirement party for Emma's mom's friend at work, another librarian. They'd like us to do something pretty. . . . There are your fondant roses, Mia! And that about wraps it up. Anything else?"

Katie nodded and held up a sheet of paper torn from a magazine. "I want to try this new pink-lemonade frosting. It's supposed to be delicious, and it might be cute for a light, floral spring cupcake."

Alexis noted it, and we all agreed. Then there was a pause, and Mia looked up with a devilish grin. "Can we just gossip now for a minute about the number-one topic in town?"

Alexis groaned and put her hands over her eyes. "When will it end?!" she cried.

Katie and I grinned at each other. "Do you have a new scoop?" I asked Mia.

"No! I thought you might, of all people, since you're so buddy-buddy with Romaine!"

The topic of the town was that Romaine Ford, our one and only homegrown superstar—model turned actress, singer, Oscar winner, and more—is premiering her new movie right here in Maple Grove in just a week! Already shopkeepers are offering premiere promotions and decorating their store windows like it's the Academy Awards. It's sort of annoying because everyone acts like they're Romaine Ford's best friend, or like she shops at their stores all the time, which they aren't and she doesn't. Even the local paper has been going around and interviewing people about her, who I'm sure don't even know her, which drives me nuts.

I, on the other hand, do know Romaine Ford.

I don't know her well, but we are *almost* what you might call friends. It's kind of a long story, but I met her when I was modeling bridesmaid dresses at the store where she bought her wedding gown. Then my friends and I made cupcakes for her wedding shower, and she came to my talent show at camp. That was a pretty big deal. We haven't stayed in touch or anything, but

I know if we were walking past each other on the street and I said, "Hi, Romaine!" she'd say, "Hi, Emma!" back.

I'm sure I will have more information tomorrow since I'm working at The Special Day bridal salon, which I do every other weekend, modeling dresses and helping out. Tomorrow she'll be coming in for a dress fitting with her bridesmaids, and I'll be delivering the salon's weekly cupcake order and staying on to help Mona, the owner of the store. The only thing is, as an employee, I'm always sworn to secrecy about brides (especially Romaine!) and their details. This can be frustrating and hard, since I'm so used to telling my friends everything. It's just that I'm so dying to tell them I'm seeing Romaine tomorrow that I might burst! I looked down at my nails. If Alexis were to look at my face, she'd totally know I was hiding something.

Since our Cupcake business meeting was finished for the day, we moved into the kitchen to start baking, and our conversation continued as we ran down all the things we knew about Romaine Ford's new movie. It's a love story, set in the past, with a lot of other famous stars, all of whom are coming to the red carpet premiere at the theater where my friends and I usually hang out! It's so insane! It's like a dream to think these actors and actresses will be here, maybe even sitting in my usual favorite seat; seventh row from the front, second seat in on the left. There will be tons of press and other Hollywood bigwigs there, plus of course Romaine Ford's handsome fiancé, the gorgeous Liam Carey, an actor and director who does all sorts of volunteer work in Africa in his spare time.

"We should try to go and watch them on the red carpet!" suggested Katie, the most starstruck of us all.

"Yes!" agreed Mia. "And we can get dressed up!"

We all laughed since Mia the fashionista will look for any excuse to get decked out.

"I can wear my dress from Dylan's sweet sixteen," said Alexis decisively, and we all laughed again since Alexis is usually so reluctant to get dressed up.

"Okay, let's focus on work for a minute," I said. I couldn't keep talking about Romaine Ford and not spill the beans. "We need to make five dozen mini cupcakes for Mona—she wants half of the vanilla-vanilla combo and half cinnamon bun with cream cheese frosting for tomorrow morning. And that's it, right?"

"Yes, but do you guys mind if I make this pink-lemonade frosting right now on the side? Maybe make an extra half dozen cupcakes and we can sample it?" asked Katie.

"Yum! Sample what?" said my oldest brother, Sam, walking into the kitchen from the mudroom.

"Sam!" cried my friends, which was both heart-warming and annoying. I have two older brothers, Sam and Matt, and one younger one, Jake, and they are all pretty irritating to me (Sam the least, actually), but my friends adore them. Mia and Katie baby Jake, Alexis is practically dating Matt, who's a year older than us, and Mia and Katie both have massive crushes on Sam (who I do have to admit is good-looking).

"Sample nothing, mister!" I scolded.

"Emma!" chided Mia.

"My brand-new pink-lemonade frosting. I don't care what Emma says—you're our official tester," declared Katie.

"No way!" I protested. "These guys will eat anything. Just slather some frosting on an old shoe, and Sam and the other guys will wolf it down and say it's delicious. They're totally indiscriminating!"

Sam came over and gave me a noogie while I shrieked. Then Matt came in with Jake, and suddenly it seemed there were boys everywhere, peering into bowls and sniffing the air.

"Out!" I commanded. "It's my kitchen time! We'll call you back if there's something to sample, okay? You're like a pack of wild hounds."

Jake and Matt howled and woofed like wild hounds, but they all finally left, with my friends in varying degrees of the giggles. It was very quiet once the boys were gone, at least in the kitchen, but I could still hear them horsing around in the den. We worked in silence for a minute, and then the conversation turned, of course, back to Romaine.

"When is she getting married?" asked Katie.

"I don't know," I said. "I would figure it's probably within the next month or two; it was a while ago that she ordered the dress." *And since she's coming in for her fitting tomorrow,* I added silently. The fitting is when they hem and alter the dress so it fits perfectly. Most brides have a few fittings close to the wedding day to make sure the dress is just right. Some are really picky and have, like, five or six, but most have around three. I knew Romaine was only having two fittings due to her schedule, so her wedding must be soon.

I kind of felt bad for Romaine. Most brides came in for their fittings with some friends and family, and it was always like a little party. Mona was coordinating how to sneak Romaine into the store so no one would try to take pictures or bother her. Trying to keep quiet like this makes me realize how hard it must be to be famous, with so many people caring about your every move. Imagine if someone was taking a picture of you every time you went to the supermarket or out to eat. I know they pay stars a lot, but really, they are never actually off duty. Work is full time and for life, if they do it well.

We finished up our baking duties, and Katie's pink-lemonade frosting turned out really well. It was a pretty, pale pink color and tasted exactly like lemonade.

"Come and get it, troops!" Katie hollered out the kitchen door, and then there was a stampede. The girls and I stood back while my brothers gorged themselves on the extra cupcakes with either lemonade or vanilla frosting.

I rolled my eyes. "Are they good?" I asked loudly.

"Umm-hmmm." Matt nodded emphatically.

"Yesss!" said Jake as crumbs tumbled out of his mouth.

"The vanilla are delicious. A little plain. The lemonade . . . ," said Sam.

Uh-oh. *He won't really say something mean about*

Katie's new frosting, will he? I worried, but I didn't need to. Good old Sammy.

"The lemonade ones are insane!"

Katie beamed like she was being photographed at a movie premiere. "Thanks!" she said happily.

I bit my tongue to keep from saying anything again about Sam not being very picky. I wanted Katie to enjoy the compliment.

"Any more?" asked Matt after eating two. He looked all around the counter to see if we were hiding some.

"That's it, mister. You can't eat up all our profits!" teased Alexis.

"I'll pay!" said Matt, reaching into his pocket.

"Oh please. Like you can afford our cupcakes!" said Alexis, swatting him with a dish towel.

"Well, maybe if you didn't charge one hundred dollars per cupcake," teased Matt. They were both laughing and looking at each other all googly-eyed, and I wanted to barf so I had to turn away. Sometimes it's superfun and convenient to have your best friend like your brother, and other times it's superannoying.

For example, later that night, all the Cupcakers went to my room to change into our pj's before we watched a movie downstairs. But this time Alexis refused to change into her pj's. I thought it was odd, but then I got it. She didn't want to wear her pj's in front of Matt.

It's just little stuff like that that adds up. I'd never say anything to Alexis though because then she would be sorry but also a little mad, and I wouldn't want to start all that up. I had enough trouble with trying to keep my bridal salon work a secret from my friends, never mind alienating them officially.

Sometimes it's so complicated just being me that I can't imagine how Romaine Ford is her.

Want more

CUPCAKE DIARIES?

Visit **CupcakeDiariesBooks.com**
for the series trailer, excerpts, activities,
and everything you need for throwing
your own cupcake party!

Coco Simon always dreamed of opening a cupcake bakery but was afraid she would eat all of the profits. When she's not daydreaming about cupcakes, Coco edits children's books and has written close to one hundred books for children, tweens, and young adults, which is a lot less than the number of cupcakes she's eaten. Cupcake Diaries is the first time Coco has mixed her love of cupcakes with writing.

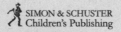